BLOODLINE

Jenn Alexander

Bywater BOOKS

2024

*For my friends, who have all made
my life so weird and wonderful.*

Empty

Edith McLean had thought that the day her parents died would forever be the worst day of her life, but as she watched the movers carry in a three-foot-tall black wooden altar with a bright red pentacle painted over the top surface, the stand carved to look as though it were being overrun by rats, she felt suddenly certain that the worst was yet to come.

"Rent is $400, and it's due on the first of each month," Edie said.

"Sure thing." Empty Jones pulled a wad of twenty-dollar bills from her pocket. "Here you go."

Empty's inner arm was dotted with needle marks in various stages of bruising, but she seemed sober enough and Edie was desperate, so she took the cash, quickly counted the $400, and then pocketed the money while running down the mental list of bills to determine which ones she absolutely *had* to pay now and which ones could wait a little longer. She'd received three notices from her electric company threatening to cut off power to her apartment, and the bank was threatening to repossess her family's coffee shop if she didn't make a mortgage payment soon. She'd already called her home, car, and business insurance companies

1

to remove all extras, opting for the most basic packages available, and even though they covered basically nothing anymore, she was hoping to avoid canceling them all together. Her landlord, with his obvious crush, would *maaaybe* forgive late rent if she brought him a coffee and touched his arm when she said good morning, though even he was souring to her excuses, and she could probably continue to siphon internet off her neighbors for another week or so before they caught on and changed the password again.

"What's your stance on séances?"

Edie blinked.

Empty stood still and serious, awaiting a reply.

When Edie had first received the email response to her "roommate wanted" ad, she'd been so relieved that it hadn't even occurred to her to ask for references. She'd wondered what the hell kind of name *Empty* was, but she hadn't given that thought enough weight, because it was clear to her now that Empty was the chosen name one takes when one is the type of person who feels it necessary to ask new roommates about a séance policy.

"Just, if you find out that this place is overrun with ghosts, don't ask them how they died. I have enough trouble sleeping without knowing if this place is haunted by some dude who had a heart attack while jerking it in the bathtub."

Empty nodded and said, "that's fair," as though they were talking about who got which shelf in the fridge.

She's definitely *going to murder me in my sleep*, Edie thought as she handed over her spare key. *I'm going to be used as a sacrifice in some sort of blood ritual.*

"Where do you want this?" Two movers stood in the entryway holding what appeared to be a coffin, and Empty went with them to show them exactly where to set it.

Either I'm going to end up in that thing, or this girl has an embalmed relative that's moving in with her, like this place is the Bates Motel and I'm in a real-life version of the movie, Psycho. Edie rubbed her temples to stave off the headache that threatened as her mind flashed to the infamous shower scene.

She looked around her living room at the boxes of open belongings that Empty had begun unpacking—a set of metal goblets with skeleton hands extending up the base; a bright red wax candle inside a skull-shaped holder, with some of the wax beginning to drip out of the skeletal eye sockets; and tattered copies of *Twilight*, *Salem's Lot*, and *Dracula*—and she hoped her new roommate's obsession with all things dead and undead didn't go too far beyond books and decor.

Ultimately, though, Empty could be practicing ritual animal sacrifice in her room, and it wouldn't have made much difference. Edie needed the cash. She went to her room, closed the door, and counted the money once more. It wasn't enough, but it was a start—enough to make a dent in the massive debt she'd inherited. She'd stop at the bank on her way to work to deposit the cash and pay her electric bill.

She yawned and crawled into bed. It was nearly noon, but Edie was hoping to get a short nap in before she had to go in to work the late shift at the coffee shop. She'd worked the early morning shift, come home to welcome Empty into the apartment and catch a short bit of sleep, and later she'd go back to staff the place until closing time.

As soon as she closed her eyes, she was jarred upright by squealing guitar; a steady *thump, thump, thump,* of bass; and screaming vocals, which all blended to create a horrific cacophony of sounds. Her immediate instinct was to go check to make sure somebody wasn't *actually* being murdered in Empty's room.

She sighed and climbed out of bed.
She wasn't going to be getting any sleep.

Capitalism, Identity, and the Yelp Reviews

The McLean Family Coffee Shop had a terrible name and terrible decor, but it was located on the corner of campus and stayed open until midnight, so it happened to be the perfect place for late-night cram sessions, and its loyal student customer base had kept the shop afloat. Barely.

Edie looked up at the hand-carved wooden sign her grandfather had made, which hung crooked above the front door. "It's in our blood" a slogan just below the shop name read.

How many times had she heard that slogan growing up? *"Coffee's in our blood, Edie,"* her dad would say. That may have been true, but business sense was not. Edie was the fourth-generation McLean to inherit The McLean Family Coffee Shop, and it appeared as though she had inherited little more than four generations' worth of business mistakes and bad purchases. Her parents, for instance, hadn't bothered to repaint the faded and chipped letters on the shop sign, or replace the pillow seats that were tearing away from the wooden chair frames. They *had*, however, recently bought a brand new twenty-five-kilo coffee roaster for $67,549 so that they could apparently roast massive commercial amounts of beans at once, replacing their perfectly functional five-kilo roaster.

"Look at this beauty," her dad had said as the roaster had been installed in the back of the shop. "We're going to really be able to expand our business with this. Just think of how many beans we can roast now."

His excitement had been contagious, and Edie hadn't been involved in the business side of the shop, so she had appropriately "oohed" and "aahed" over the fancy roasting machine. Now, though, she looked at the mound of debt and the backlog of unsold roasted beans, and she could muster nothing but anger toward the giant roasting monstrosity her parents had thought to spend every last dime, and then some, on.

If she didn't love the place so damn much, she would just let the bank take it, except the shop, for all of its flaws and shortcomings, had been her childhood home. She grew up helping her parents unpack the pallets of unroasted beans, taste-testing the various latte flavor combinations they came up with and staying up past her bedtime to chat with all the customers.

It's in our blood.

Edie couldn't let the bank take the place. She had to save it.

She stepped inside and breathed in the smell of freshly brewed coffee, letting the familiar scent soothe her for a minute before she had to get to work.

"Hey boss. Can I make you a coffee?"

She looked at her employee Blake with more love than she'd ever have for any other guy. "I would *love* one."

He nodded and set to work, grinding the beans to set in the ceramic pour-over carafe.

"It seems we're both in a state of morphogenesis right now," he mused while he waited for the hot water to boil.

"Yeah, I suppose so." Edie was unsure exactly what she was agreeing to, but then she didn't understand most of what Blake said to her. She'd long-since learned not to ask for an explanation if she wasn't ready for an hour-long philosophy lecture. Blake's entire career ambition seemed to be to debate the meaning of life over the perfect cup of coffee, which made him an invaluable member of the McLean Family Coffee Shop's staff. She'd had to lay off nearly her entire team due to their dire financial situation, but Blake was the last employee she'd ever let go.

"If you had to triage this place, what would you fix first?" Edie asked.

"I don't know." Blake looked around as though taking in the details for the first time, and then he shrugged. "This place has a certain charm to it."

Edie didn't disagree. She found the floral-print chair cushions to be a little quirky, but soothing, and she thought that the family photos on the walls demonstrated a personal touch, showing all the love that had gone into the coffee shop. However, the place had looked the same for approximately fifty years and held little appeal to anyone without a personal connection to it. She wasn't naive. She knew what people said. She'd read the Yelp reviews.

College students had nicknamed the place "Bloodline Coffee" because of their slogan and because they only ever visited when they wanted caffeine injected straight into their bloodstream.

She watched as Blake poured the boiling water from the long-necked pour-over kettle onto the ground beans, mesmerized by the steady drip of coffee as it filled the clear carafe below.

"Fun fact: prior to modern capitalism, the concept of

7

personal identity didn't really exist," Blake said.

Edie blinked as she tried to understand where he was going with this turn in conversation.

"Capitalism caused a shift away from group identity toward more individualistic identity, and work is often viewed as a manifestation of individual identity. So, if you're asking what to do with the coffee shop, I suppose I would ask you to consider that people often identify with their careers, and I'd ask if this place is an appropriate representation of you?"

Edie took the cup of coffee as he slid it across the counter. The barely functioning mess of a shop actually felt like the perfect representation of her at the moment, but she didn't want to admit that to Blake.

"I'll swing by Home Depot first thing in the morning and pick up some paint," Edie said. "I'll start by fixing the lettering out front."

A Band-Aid on a huge gaping wound.

But it was *something* at least.

She took a few minutes to finish her coffee and settle herself for her evening shift, and then she set to work filling customer orders, bouncing between the counter and the walk-up window her grandparents had insisted had been popular back in their day, but which only seemed to confuse millennials who were used to being able to drive up to take-out windows.

Since her parents' death, Edie had been burning the candle at both ends, working a split shift at the coffee shop, where she opened at 5:00 a.m. until 9:00 a.m., and then returned in the evening to work from 5:00 p.m. until midnight. It meant she didn't need to retain two sets of staff and could have a single pair cover the daytime hours. It also meant she got little-to-no sleep, but that seemed like a small price to pay to keep the shop alive. The opening shifts were a certain kind of hell as she pulled herself groggily from her bed far before she was ready each day, but she didn't mind closing. There was a subdued energy in the evenings. Most customers weren't looking for the immediate caffeine boost to start their days, and so they didn't tend to rush in and out. Students came in and sat down to talk about class, or crack textbooks and study together. She looked forward to the presence of the writing group that met on Mondays, the Dungeon & Dragons band that met on Wednesdays, and the Thursday night crochet club. There was a greater feeling of connectivity in the evenings, and while the place perhaps didn't have the mass appeal of the Jimmies that now dotted every corner, it fit a cozy little community niche.

A knock at the walk-up window pulled her from her musings, and Edie turned, instantly brightening.

"You're here early."

The woman on the other side of the window smiled and shrugged one shoulder—a move that made Edie swoon a little. "It's a nice night out. I thought I'd take my time on my walk to work. Enjoy the fresh air."

Edie didn't know the woman's name, even though she'd been frequenting the coffee shop for the past couple of months. She'd been too tongue-tied to ask. She was certain that she'd open her mouth to ask and what would come out instead was "Marry me and have my babies." All she knew was that the woman worked as a nurse at the hospital a block over, and that she bought the other night-shift staff coffees on a near-nightly basis.

"The usual?" Edie asked, cursing herself for not making more conversation.

"Please." The way she said the single word made Edie blush as her mind immediately conjured images of much more fun scenarios where she might hear that word.

She nodded once, took a breath that didn't seem to fill her lungs, and set to work filling four to-go cups with coffee, and tucking cream and sugar packets between the beverages on the tray. Then she handed the tray of coffee through the window while imagining the softness of the woman's porcelain skin, which appeared flawless beneath the dim glow of the shop lights.

"You know," Edie blurted, "you should come in and sit down for a coffee one of these days."

The woman smiled and leaned in as she said, "Maybe you'll properly invite me in sometime."

Edie didn't know what to say to the strange reply, though she was fairly certain it had been said in a flirtatious manner. Was she waiting for Edie to ask her out? Should she take the chance? Was she going to humiliate herself and never see this woman again?

"Thanks for the coffee," the night-shift nurse said, and she smiled in a way that twisted Edie's stomach in knots.

Edie managed to stammer an awkward "Have a good night" before the woman was gone and she was left standing at the window with a silly half-grin on her face.

"You should ask her whether she conscribes to dualism or materialism," Blake said. "I always find that to be an effective icebreaker and a good way to get to know somebody. And if she doesn't know what you're asking about, you can save yourself a great deal of time from the start."

"Thanks," Edie said, "but I think I'll start by asking her name." Then she added a wistful "One of these days."

Obsidian and Other
Shades of Black

Edie sat at her dining room table, eating scrambled eggs and flipping through the Home Depot catalog of paint colors when suddenly there was a lanky guy with pale skin and long, greasy black hair, dressed only in a pair of boxer briefs that left little to the imagination, going through her cupboards.

"Where do you keep the cereal?" He asked the question as though he wasn't mostly naked, speaking to a stranger for the first time.

Edie had heard voices in Empty's room the night before, which was the only reason she didn't immediately pick up her phone to call the police, and even then she rested her fingertips on it. Just in case things got any weirder.

"I don't eat cereal," Edie said. "Also, we haven't met. I'm Edith."

"Sid." He didn't take his eyes off the open cupboard. "Who doesn't eat cereal?"

Empty chose that moment to enter the kitchen, and she wrapped her arms around Sid's waist, kissing him up the neck.

Edie coughed, feeling the need to assert her presence.

"Sorry, Edie," Empty said. She kept her arms wrapped around Sid. "I meant to introduce you to Obsidian last night, but you were working late, and by the time you got home we were deep into a movie."

Obsidian and Empty. What a pair.

"All good," Edie said, and turned back to her eggs, the one normal part of her morning.

"Add Cap'n Crunch to our shopping list," Sid said, and he opened the bag of nine-grain bread that Edie had splurged on at the local bakery, popping three whole slices into the toaster.

Add Sharpie to mine, Edie thought, as she made a mental note to put her name on all her food items. She could barely afford to feed herself, let alone Empty and her boyfriend.

Edie went back to the color catalog, her eyes crossing as she tried to decipher one shade of black from the next, and then it occurred to her that Empty with her all-black wardrobe was probably the expert she needed.

"Which shade of black looks the most professional? I'm repainting the coffee shop sign, but these all look the same to me."

Empty moved to study the catalog over Edie's shoulder, and she "hmm'ed" with way more seriousness than the task warranted as she looked over her options.

"I was thinking maybe jet black," Edie said. "That's, like, the blackest you can get, right?"

"Are you even looking at the palette?" Empty asked. "If you want a really bold black, I'd suggest you go with onyx."

Edie looked at onyx and she looked at jet black. Any difference was indecipherable.

"You're right. Onyx it is. Thanks."

"I was meaning to ask you," Empty began, and the cautious segue immediately sounded alarm bells in Edie's brain. "What evenings are you home?"

Edie felt the sudden need to stay home every evening and keep eyes on her apartment, but she had nobody else to work closing shift.

"Maybe tonight, if repainting the sign doesn't run late." It was Sunday, the only day of the week that the shop was closed.

"And the rest of the week?"

"I'll be working late," Edie admitted. "I'll be home after midnight."

She could see that Empty was deep in thought, and she immediately recalled Empty inquiring about her stance on séances. She *hoped* a séance was all that Empty had planned, but somehow didn't think she was quite so lucky.

"Don't worry," Sid interjected. "We're simply having a friend over for drinks. A little weekly ritual we have. No big deal."

She'd just met Sid, but somehow, him telling her that it was no big deal told her that it was a *very* big deal. She reminded herself of the $400 that Empty was willing to pay on time and in cash, and she kept silent.

"All good. Do your thing," Edie said.

"Thanks," Empty replied.

"Don't mention it." Edie had never meant those words more.

She finished her eggs and cleared her plate from the table. She had a million and one items on her to-do list, but she wanted an hour to relax and watch something mindless on Netflix before heading back to Home Depot to pick up a can of onyx paint so she could repaint the letters on the damn sign. Her television called to her as she walked past her living room, which no longer felt like her own.

13

Her room was her one remaining sanctuary, and she sat down on her bed to watch Netflix on her laptop. Instead, she picked up the photo of her parents that sat next to her computer on her nightstand. It was a photo she'd snapped when they'd joined her at the pride parade the previous summer. Her parents stood smiling brightly with the sun in their eyes. Her dad had his arm around her mom's shoulder. They wore matching shirts that said, "I love my daughter," transposed over top of a giant rainbow heart. They'd always epitomized unconditional love.

And a few months later their lives had ended when their little environmentally conscious car had been hit by a sixteen-wheeler whose long-haul driver had nodded off at the wheel. Just like that. Alive one minute, dead the next.

She felt tears burn behind her eyelids, but she refused to let them fall. After the funeral, she hadn't cried for her parents once with the pressure of keeping the shop afloat stealing her grief from her. She didn't have the luxury of falling apart.

"It's in our blood, Edie."

She thought about what Blake had said about work and identity. The coffee shop didn't just belong to her family; it *was* her family. Her parents had lived and breathed that coffee shop. Her grandparents had lived and breathed that coffee shop. Her great-grandparents had lived and breathed that coffee shop.

It couldn't die along with her parents. She had to keep it alive.

"I'm going to find a way to turn things around, Dad," she promised.

She set the photo down and picked up her laptop, but she didn't open Netflix. Instead, she watched YouTube painting tutorials, and then she headed to the hardware store.

14

Nothing Good Ever Comes in Comic Sans

Edie hadn't thought that the prep work and research for sign painting would be an all-day affair, but by the time she got back to the McLean Family Coffee Shop with her paint and supplies, the sun was already setting. Then, getting the sign down proved to be a challenge and a half.

"One fucking win," Edie mumbled, as she balanced on the ladder and pounded the wooden monstrosity as though that would loosen the stubborn final screw. "That's all I want."

"You look like you could use a hand."

Edie nearly lost her balance as she spun to see who had spoken, and embarrassment flooded her face at the sight of her favorite night-shift nurse, standing below in the yellow sodium-vapor glow of the streetlights, gray eyes shining with amusement.

"I've almost got it, but thanks."

"Mmhmm. I can see that." The woman stood back, hands on her hips as she took in Edie's failure with a playful smirk.

Edie struggled to find the humor in the situation. *All the things I've lost this year, and now I get to lose my pride and any*

15

remaining appearance of competence as well.

"Let me give it a try," the woman said at Edie's next failed attempt.

Edie shook her head, but she had already begun to climb down the ladder.

"It's really stuck."

The woman held out her hand for the screwdriver.

"Don't say I didn't warn you."

She watched as the woman climbed the ladder, her gaze lingering selfishly as it trailed her backside.

"You're not wearing your scrubs," Edie noted as her eyes followed the way the woman's plaid shirt clung to her sides, disappearing where it was tucked into dark jeans that hugged the very subtle curve of hips.

"It's my night off," the woman said. "I live a block over and wanted to get some fresh air. Here you go."

Before Edie could get her mind around what was happening, she had a metal screw in her hand, and she was watching as the woman carried the wooden sign down the ladder.

Her face flamed as her remaining pride went down the drain.

"Thanks," she stammered.

The woman gave a lazy one-shoulder shrug, which was way too attractive for something so humiliating.

"I'm Penny, by the way."

We're doing this. We're introducing ourselves. I finally get to officially meet the woman I've been crushing on for months, and it's while I'm standing here looking like a total fool.

"Edie." Her name came out with a grimace, as in that moment she wished she could be literally anyone else.

"So why are you taking your sign down, anyway, Edie?"

16

Penny asked. "You're not closing, are you?"

Not yet anyway. "The sign needs some touch-ups. I thought I'd repaint the letters, but I didn't realize the project would turn into a full day and night affair. I thought it would be a quick fix."

"I can help."

"No," Edie said. "I can't ask you to do that."

"You're not asking. I'm offering. Come on, it sounds like fun."

A root canal sounded like more fun, but Edie didn't say as much. Instead, she said, "Well, who am I to stand in the way of your fun?"

"That's the spirit."

Edie opened the door and held it for Penny, who remained rooted in place.

"Come on in," Edie said, and the words unglued Penny's feet from the sidewalk.

Penny carried the sign in, and Edie went to the table where she'd set all her paint supplies. She opened up the package with the plastic drop-sheet and spread that over the table before laying out the rest of the items.

Penny placed the sign on the table, and Edie stood, really taking it in for the first time: The juvenile font shouting at the street-front in all caps, the cumbersome name and the silly slogan, the peeling paint that clearly had never stayed within the lines of the letters in the first place.

THE McLEAN FAMILY COFFEE SHOP
It's in our blood!

The sign was a tragedy. Probably, so was the shop.

Nothing good ever comes in comic sans, she thought as she

17

gazed down at the gaudy lettering. Paint was only going to get them so far.

"I hope I don't need a primer," Edie said, lifting the can of *Onyx* paint onto the table and prying it open.

"You'll be fine," Penny promised. She had already reached for the sandpaper, and she began filing the letters. Edie watched as her hands moved expertly in smooth circles over the shop name. The peeling paint fell away, leaving smooth wood with mottled color behind.

"You seem to know what you're doing."

Another one-shoulder shrug. "When you're as old as me, you pick up a few skills."

Edie laughed. "You can't be that much older than I am. How old are you? Twenty-seven? Twenty-eight?"

"Sure, we'll go with that," Penny said, leaving Edie's curiosity piqued.

She opened the can of paint and used a wooden stir stick to mix it up, before setting the paint next to the sign and pulling out the brushes. She'd bought a handful of different sizes, unsure which would be best for hand-painting all the shop letters.

Penny picked up one of the finer brushes and began tracing the edges of the letters, and Edie followed suit.

"So," Penny said, dragging out the word, "The McLean Family Coffee Shop. Is that your family?"

"It is," Edie said, wishing the sense of pride she felt was actually warranted. "My great-grandfather opened this coffee shop. After coming home from World War II, he said he wanted to do something that made people happy, and what made people happier than a good cup of coffee?"

"Smart man."

"I don't think he really knew much about the business, but

18

he poured his heart into it, and he learned a lot about coffee roasting, even if his business sense was lacking."

"Everyone I've talked to in town agrees that there *is* something about the coffee here that's special," Penny said.

Edie looked up and met her gray eyes. "Thank you for saying that."

Penny held her gaze. "It's the truth."

It was a long moment before Edie looked back down to the sign, dipping her brush in the paint and beginning to trace another letter.

"If only a talent for coffee roasting was all this place needed," Edie said. "The McLean family is a family of really abysmal business people."

Penny laughed as though Edie was hyperbolizing, but when she noticed Edie not laughing along, she quickly sobered. "How bad is it?"

"The place is pretty much bankrupt," Edie admitted. "I just lost my parents, and I'm desperately trying to not lose this place, too. It turns out my parents thought the solution to having no money was to spend money. They bought a commercial-sized roaster with absolutely no distribution plan, and now I'm left with that debt on top of their prior debt."

Edie stopped and inhaled a deep cleansing breath at the end of her emotional unloading.

"Oof," Penny said, taking in the heaviness.

"Sorry. That was a lot."

"So you stepped in and took over?" Penny asked.

"Yeah," Edie said. "It was always a given that I'd be running this place one day, but I didn't think it would be nearly so soon. I'd just gone to Peru, where I meant to spend some time learning about coffee from the source, when I got the call. I dropped

19

everything, and now here we are."

"Painting this sign together," Penny finished.

The letters were nearly done, and the sign looked miles better already.

"I really appreciate your help. I want to say I could have done it on my own, but . . ." Edie trailed off.

"You'd still be up on that ladder."

"I'd still be up on that ladder," Edie agreed.

Penny finished painting the final couple of letters.

"Let me make you a latte or something before you leave," Edie said.

Penny shook her head. "I'm good, but thanks."

"I know you always order the drip coffee, but I'll make you something special. Do you like macadamia nut?"

"I really can't."

Edie sensed that their time together had ended, but she ached to stretch out the evening just a little longer.

"Have dinner with me," she blurted, and she watched, a tangle of optimism and anxiety, as Penny considered the offer.

Penny chewed on her inner cheek before saying, "I'm sorry, but no."

Edie let out the breath she'd been holding. She'd been trying to find the courage to ask Penny out for the past couple of months. Now she had, and the worst-case scenario was playing out, the sting of rejection made worse by the fact that she had really thought they'd connected over the course of the evening.

"Do you work tomorrow evening?" Penny asked. "I dabble in night sky photography, and I was thinking of driving out to the dark sky preserve tomorrow to take some photos. Would you want to join?"

Edie's chest lifted at the realization that the rejection was of dinner, not of her, but her elation was quickly dashed as she had to decline the offer. "I have to work closing shift. I'll be stuck here until midnight."

"Why don't I pick you up then?"

"You want to pick me up at *midnight*?" Edie asked.

That sexy one-shoulder shrug. Edie could practice and never look half as cool.

"I work night shift, remember? Your midnight is my noon."

Edie would be exhausted at work the following day, but she eagerly agreed to the date. "I'm in."

Penny smiled and got up from the table, taking one last look at their handiwork.

"Get some sleep, Edie," she said. "I'll pick you up here at midnight tomorrow."

Edie walked with Penny to the door. "I can't wait," she said.

She watched as Penny disappeared into the night, and then she began turning off all the lights in the store so that she could go home and get some sleep. Her 4:00 a.m. alarm was going to come way too soon, and she wanted to be rested if she was going to go on a date after work.

A date. With Penny.

She looked at the sign, grateful in that moment for every one of its flaws. Without that sign, she'd still be serving coffees to Penny, trying to work up the courage to ask her name.

Maybe my luck is finally about to turn, Edie thought.

The Self-Indulgent Suffering of Fools

"I'll have a large black coffee," the man said, adjusting his wiry glasses. "Your strongest brew. It's going to be a long night."

"I was going to ask how your novel was going," Edie said, "but . . ."

"Don't."

Edie tamped down her delight. When things were going well for the members of the writing group, they tended to keep their heads down, fingers on the keyboard, and then they went home early. When things were not going well, they tended to stay late and order lots of coffee while distracting their peers under the guise of crowd-sourcing ideas. It only took one writer with writer's block to shift the group dynamic from focused work session to highly caffeinated social hour.

"I've been working on developing a backstory for each of my characters, and there's some dark history between the Orcs and the Elves. It's going to make for rich characters, but I'm going to have to do some heavy rewriting toward the beginning of the book if I want to make it plausible that my two main characters, who happen to be an Orc and an Elf, would even think to embark on this quest together in the first place. And there's *no way* they would be traveling together without some significant tension, so I can't write them like best friends anymore, which changes the entire dynamic of the book."

"That sounds like a lot of work," Edie offered, as she poured the man his coffee. *Fuel up.*

Then an idea came to her.

"There's a Dungeons and Dragons group that meets here on Wednesday nights. You should come back then and talk to them. Maybe they'll have some insight."

The look of surprise and delight on the man's face told Edie the suggestion had been a good one. "Do you think they'd be willing to talk with me? They would be the exact audience for this book. Their feedback would be invaluable."

In Edie's experience, the members of the role-playing game had endless enthusiasm for fantasy storytelling. They'd be thrilled to help untangle the plot of a real-life fantasy novel.

"Come again Wednesday and I'll introduce you," Edie said. She poured the man a mug of coffee and slid it across the counter to him.

"Thank you," he said, and the emphasis he gave the words told Edie he was thanking her for more than the coffee.

"Just be sure to mention this place when your book is famous," Edie said.

That was when the idea came to her.

She watched him take his coffee back to the table where his writing friends had begun to gather, and she said to Blake, "Do you think Ellora Merriweather would help us promote this place?"

"Who?" Blake asked.

Edie studied him, trying to determine whether he was serious, or if his ignorance was feigned as some pretentious show.

"The romance author," she said. "You know, our city's one claim to fame."

Blake had a blank look on his face and seemed genuinely clueless enough. "I don't read romance."

"And I don't read horror, but I know who Stephen King is."

"Who?"

Edie blew out a breath of frustration. "You're shitting me. You have to be shitting me."

Blake shrugged lazily. "I don't read fiction. I tend to find fiction to be nothing more than the self-indulgent suffering of fools."

This earned looks from the writing group, who had clearly overheard. One or two of them appeared ready to come over and try to enlighten Blake. It would be a wasted effort.

"Whatever," Edie said. "She's famous and she's local. If she put a good word for us out into the world, it would probably make a huge impact on our business."

"Does she come here often?" Blake asked.

Edie shook her head.

"Does she come here at all?"

Edie deflated and shook her head again.

Blake leaned back and considered everything. "I'm not a statistician, but even so I'd say the odds are vastly unlikely, though I admire your optimism."

"You're right." Edie hated to admit that for so many reasons.

She'd seen the freshly painted sign at the start of her shift, and the sight of it, so much improved, had inflated both her confidence and her drive. But the reality was, she still had a ton of debt, and it was going to take more than some touched-up letters on a wooden sign to save the place.

Edie pulled out the notebook where she kept her running to-do list, and she added "try to contact Ellora Merriweather about promotion." Her optimism may have been foolish and misplaced, but it felt like *something*. The rest of the items on the list ("fix chairs," "repaint the interior walls," "sell more coffee") all felt either too minimal or too vague to really help the place.

The next time she had some downtime at home, she would look into how she might be able to contact Ms. Merriweather.

Not tonight, though. Tonight, I have a date!

Even watching her family's legacy die a slow death couldn't take away from that excitement. It was a bright spot amid all the darkness that was her life these days. She was watching the clock and counting down until midnight when Penny would come pick her up for their stargazing excursion.

Edie swooned a little at the thought. It was the first thing she'd had to look forward to in ages.

Bold Streak

Edie turned the key to lock the coffee shop for the night when she heard the throaty growl of the rusty blue pickup truck as it rolled up behind her.

"Nice sign." Penny leaned across the center console to call out to Edie through the open passenger-side window.

"You know, I didn't get half as many compliments on it today as I thought I would. It's almost as though nobody noticed our hard work, and that just doesn't seem right."

"How could they not?" Penny asked. "We poured hours of our life into that beauty."

"It's the highlight of the entire street if you ask me."

"Oh, I agree."

Penny got out of the truck, and Edie's laughter was immediately silenced by the sight in front of her. Penny was so casually cool, in a black T-shirt beneath a wool-lined denim jacket. Her hair was tied back loosely, with some dark curls falling around her face, framing her angular jaw.

"Hop in," Penny said as she opened the passenger door to the truck.

"Hang on," Edie said. She had a bag full of expired pastries, Danishes, and cinnamon rolls from the bakery down the road that she hadn't been able to resell on time and didn't want to toss in the trash. She quickly ran down the street and gave them to the man bundled on the corner before racing back to where Penny stood studying her with a tender gaze.

"I wouldn't have pegged you for the pickup truck type," Edie said, and the worn-down vehicle shifted and groaned as she lifted herself up and into the cab.

"I've had Frankie here for over ten years now." Penny patted the door frame affectionately. "I try not to stay in one place for too long, and she's helped me through a number of moves."

Doesn't stick around. Edie filed it mentally with disappointment as Penny closed the door for her and went around to the driver's seat.

"So, where are you from originally?" Edie asked, as Penny shoulder-checked and pulled the truck away from the curb.

"Originally? That was another lifetime. Most recently, Seattle."

"You moved from Seattle to *here*?" Edie's brain struggled to compute that information. "Why on earth would you do that?"

"Seattle was rad, but it was time for a change."

"It's on my bucket list of places to visit," Edie said. "One day I'll go and make the pilgrimage to the birthplace of Starbucks."

Penny chuckled. "Isn't Starbucks, like, every local coffee shop's arch nemesis?"

"Listen," Edie said, giving the question way more seriousness than was probably warranted. "The Jimmies that are popping up all over the place with their one-dollar motor-oil coffees are my nemesis. Starbucks is a chain, but at least it's known for ethical business practices and good-quality brew."

She watched as Penny tipped her head from side to side, considering her words. "That's an admirable stance."

Edie shrugged. "I'm practically bankrupt, so what do I know?"

Penny's laugh filled the car, and Edie sank back into the warmth of it as the truck turned out of the city and onto the dark highway that would lead them to the national park outside of town with its dark sky preserve.

Be careful getting into cars with strangers, Edie, her mom's voice cautioned through memory, but the reminder didn't cause alarm bells to ring within her. Rather it highlighted the irony of driving to the middle of nowhere in the middle of the night with a veritable stranger and yet feeling nothing but safe. Somehow, things with Penny were easy and comfortable. Their date was the one thing in her life that she wasn't worried about.

The lonely road stretched forward into blackness, which sucked in around them as they left the city and its light pollution behind.

"I haven't been here since I was a kid," Edie said as they drove through the entrance to the national park.

"Really?" Penny asked. "You live so close, and it's so beautiful out here. I try to get out here once a week, at least."

"Life is just busy." Edie let the last word trail off. She thought of her parents and all the things they'd talked about doing together *one day*. "There's never enough time, is there? Life goes by so fast."

"Not always," Penny said.

Edie found the response strange, and she was about to comment, but before she could think what to say, Penny said, "Here we are," and killed the headlights and the ignition and hopped out of the truck.

"Where are you going?" Edie asked.

"I can't take photos from inside the truck."

Edie looked out at the endless dark. "Aren't there animals out here?"

"We'll be fine."

Edie didn't feel reassured, but she climbed out and went around back, where Penny had spread out a small air mattress. It whirred to life as a battery pump filled it with air. Then Penny tossed a few pillows and blankets on top of the mattress and offered Edie her hand.

"Come on."

Her heart hammered at the unexpected intimacy of the evening, but she took Penny's hand and stepped up into the truck bed, sitting on the little one-inch-thick mattress while Penny arranged the pillows. The early-autumn air had a bite to it, and even with her warm jacket Edie was grateful for the blankets, which she didn't hesitate to pull across her lap.

They sat overlooking the national park's big lake. Edie's eyes had adjusted to the darkness, and even with no artificial lights, she was surprised at how bright the night was. The moon was full and heavy in the sky, and it reflected off the water, giving an almost ethereal glow to the landscape. She could make out the silhouettes of the spruce trees surrounding them. Stars peppered the sky with more density and vibrance than Edie could ever remember seeing.

Penny set up a tripod with a large DSLR camera at their feet, and then she laid down beside Edie, motioning for Edie to do the same.

Edie swallowed hard as she lay next to Penny.

"You don't have to be nervous," Penny said, as though she could hear Edie's pounding heart. "We're just looking at stars."

29

That didn't feel like a small thing, but Edie took a deep breath in and let her body relax into the mattress, trying to stay focused on the night sky and not the pretty girl lying next to her, their arms so close that it would take no more than a shiver to close the distance.

"I love it out here," Penny said, so quietly that Edie wasn't entirely sure she was speaking to her. "The night sky is so bright and beautiful that it almost makes me feel like I'm not missing out."

"Missing out?" Edie asked, rolling her head lazily to the side to gaze over at Penny, who shook her head as though she hadn't intended to speak the words.

"Working nights," she clarified. "I never expected to be on night shift. It was never what I'd planned for myself."

"How come you ended up on night shift then?"

"It's a long story" was all Penny offered.

"For what it's worth," Edie said, "it's at least led us here."

Penny reached over and took her hand, giving a gentle squeeze.

"You're freezing," Edie said, sitting up. "Let me give you my jacket."

She was already shrugging it off, but Penny tugged on her arm to pull her back down. "No, please. I'm fine."

"You feel like a corpse," Edie blurted, immediately regretting the words.

You feel like a corpse? Real sexy. No wonder you're single.

"I run a little cold, that's all."

Edie frowned over at her, but she didn't look uncomfortable, so Edie settled back down and took Penny's hand in her own once again. Penny's hand was unnaturally cold, but still her own skin warmed when Penny traced her thumb over the back of her hand.

"Do you know much about the different constellations?" Penny asked.

"I know there's a Big Dipper and a Little Dipper, but I couldn't point them out to you."

"My favorite is Andromeda, the chained woman," Penny said, and she pointed. "Over there."

Edie followed her finger, but couldn't magically make out any order to the stars above.

Penny took Edie's hand, pointed it upward, and traced the pattern with Edie's finger.

"There's her head, her torso, arms and legs. She's chained to the rock there. That star is the most distant object visible to the human eye."

Edie only distantly listened to Penny's words. She was focused instead on every point of contact where Penny's arm rested against her own.

"Do you see?" Penny asked.

Edie saw random dots, but she nodded.

The first flash of color caught them both off guard. Edie's breath caught at the sudden bold green streak that burst across the sky.

Beside her, Penny shot upright and reached for her camera. She adjusted it so that it pointed to where the green ribbon twisted and danced above them. Then she lay down, pressed a button on her remote.

The shutter clicked, again and again, while Edie and Penny lay in silence together.

Edie hadn't seen the northern lights since she was a child, and they were as breathtaking now as she remembered. Maybe more so with her adult appreciation.

She could hear Penny murmur "wow" every so often, followed

by more click, click, clicking of the camera, but otherwise the night was silent.

The odd streak of purple shocked through the brilliant green, and each time it did, a thrill shot through Edie. The entire night was electric.

As the lights began to slow and fade, Edie's focus shifted back to Penny, and she propped herself on her arm so that she could study the way Penny's eyes widened with awe.

"You smell nice," Penny said before turning her gaze to meet Edie's.

Goosebumps raised over Edie's skin at the compliment. "Do I?"

"Mmhmm," Penny answered, and she closed her eyes for a moment, breathing in deeply. "You smell like sunshine and daffodils, with the lingering scent of coffee clinging to your skin. Like morning on the front porch."

Edie's breath hitched, and she could feel the spark crackle through the air between them. She thought of the lights, rare and bold, and felt a bold streak swell within her.

She leaned down and kissed Penny, acting entirely on the moment, all of her characteristic over-thinking and anxiety silenced by desire.

When their lips met, the sparks exploded. Penny pressed herself up and into the kiss, pulling Edie's face toward her. Her hands knotted in Edie's hair, and her lips and tongue moved expertly over Edie's mouth.

Edie gasped as Penny's teeth raked across her bottom lip, before Penny sucked that lip into her mouth hard.

Edie pulled back, breathless, thirsty for air.

"You taste like morning, too," Penny said, and she folded her arms behind her head, and smiled up at Edie, who tried to control her breathing. She had never been kissed like that before in her life.

Edie lay back down beside Penny, curling against her side, her head resting on Penny's shoulder. If she kept kissing her, she was sure they wouldn't stop there, and Edie didn't sleep with people on the first date.

But whatever was building between them, it felt as rare and special as the northern lights, and Edie closed her eyes, settling into the warmth and perfection of the moment.

She hadn't realized that she'd dozed off until she felt Penny gently nudge her awake. For a brief moment, she let herself laze somewhere between sleep and wakefulness, comfortable and warm beneath the blankets in the back of Penny's truck, curled up against Penny's soft body, and then her eyes shot open.

"Shit, shit, shit, shit." She sat stark upright. "What time is it?" She was already brushing her fingers through her hair. "I'm going to be late for work." She felt unusually rested, which told her there was no way she was going to be on time to open the shop.

"Relax," Penny said, and she set a hand on Edie's shoulder to calm her, but Edie's panic was far past the point of calm.

"If I don't open, nobody will, and I can't afford to miss out on the business from the morning rush. If any of my regulars start going to Jimmies instead, I'm fucked."

"You were only asleep for an hour," Penny said. "It's only 3:30 a.m. We've got plenty of time to get you back to your coffee shop. I promise."

The words didn't immediately register, and Edie continued

her panic, running through a mental list of how she could compensate for the morning's lost income. Even a loss of $80 . . . that was her phone bill for the month.

"Edie," Penny said, "you'll be fine."

Edie stopped and looked at Penny, who set a hand on either side of Edie's face. The coolness of her touch was enough to still her racing nervous system.

"I know what time your shop opens," Penny said. "You were tired, so I let you sleep for an hour, but I knew to wake you up."

Edie's panic finally began to dissipate.

"What if you had fallen asleep, too?"

"I only sleep when the sun's up," Penny promised.

Edie's heart rate returned to normal, and as the panic abated the embarrassment set in.

"I fell asleep." She groaned, wanting to bury herself back beneath the covers. "On our first date." *Oh God. Probably our only date.*

"I enjoyed having you cuddled up against me," Penny answered. "I enjoyed every aspect of our evening immensely."

"Oh yes," Edie said with an eye roll. "A romantic evening holding a sleeping lump."

"It's been ages since anyone has slept next to me," Penny admitted. "I forgot how relaxing it is, the rise and fall of a sleeping chest. I watched the stars and held you, and it has been one of the best nights I can remember."

Edie was skeptical, but the earnestness in Penny's voice told her that Penny meant it, even if Edie still felt coils of guilt for sleeping through their date.

"We should probably get going, though," Penny said. "As much as I'd like to keep lying here next to you."

"We should," Edie agreed, regretfully.

Edie helped fold blankets while Penny deflated the little air mattress, and then she reluctantly climbed back into the passenger seat.

"I'm sorry I have to work," Edie said as Penny started the ignition. "I'd have loved to stay out here and catch the sunrise with you."

"If only that was possible," Penny said, her words wistful.

At least she seems as sad for the date to be ending as I am.

"Maybe for our second date?" Edie chanced.

The long pause made Edie's stomach twist. "We'll see."

"About the sun rise, or the second date?" Edie hated the insecurity she heard in her voice.

Penny took her eyes off the road for a moment to catch Edie's gaze.

"There will *definitely* be a second date."

Edie's held breath released, and she tried not to show how giddy that thought made her.

The park was an hour out of the city, but the drive felt like mere minutes before they were back within the city limits.

"Do you want me to drop you off at home?" Penny asked.

Edie looked at the time and shook her head. She was wearing the same clothes as the day before, but they'd have to do.

"The coffee shop is good," she said. "I'll change on my break."

Penny pulled in front of the McLean Family Coffee Shop and Edie lingered in the passenger seat, remiss for the evening to end.

"I had a great time tonight," she said. "Thank you. For everything."

Penny leaned in and kissed Edie, a light, soft kiss that promised more. Then she pulled back and said, "Go save your coffee shop, Edie. You've got this. One cup of coffee at a time."

35

Emboldened by the evening, Edie climbed out of the truck feeling for the first time in forever that anything truly was possible.

She was going to save the place.

A Quick, Wheezy Death

Edie should have been expecting the shit storm that awaited her. That was, after all, the way of her universe. For every good thing that happened to her, an equal or worse bad thing awaited. And her date with Penny had been amazing.

She'd barely slept the previous night, and still she'd gone into work motivated and energized.

You taste like morning.

The words had echoed in Edie's mind as she went to steam milk for the first latte of the day. She moved with a lightness she was unaccustomed to, and she caught herself smiling at random moments.

And then her good mood died right along with her milk steamer. It wheezed its final puffs of air, devolved into a steady high-pitched squeal, and resolutely broke with one loud clunk.

"Goddamn it," Edie cursed under her breath, before turning to apologize to the waiting customer.

She tried everything she knew about fixing electronics—she gave it a hard knock on the side, and she turned it off and then back on again—before concluding that her milk steamer had really and truly broken down.

"What did I ever do?" Edie asked the universe, as she gave the steamer one last attempt. "Did I break a mirror I'm unaware of, or walk under a ladder, or something?"

Silence answered her.

Edie pinched the bridge of her nose, and then apologized to the customer once more before refunding her money.

She could hear the money-lost tally ringing up in her head with each order she had to turn down.

"I'm sorry, our steamer is broken today. Can I interest you in an Americano? Or perhaps you'd like to try one of our drip coffees. We have a new blonde roast that is really wonderful."

She watched customer after customer walk out disappointed and empty-handed, or almost-as-bad, carrying a drip coffee for a quarter the price of their original order.

And not all of them swallowed the news politely.

"I've been in line for ten minutes," one man said, holding his briefcase in one hand and cell phone in the other, while he tapped the toe of his perfectly polished black shoes.

Edie wanted to mention that he'd have heard her deliver the news to the handful of customers ahead of him had he taken his eyes off his phone, but all she said was, "I'm really sorry."

He huffed and left without buying anything.

When there was finally a lull between customers, Edie decided to try to get ahead of the problem. She grabbed a piece of paper and a Sharpie and wrote in large letters "Our steamer has died a quick, wheezy death. Unfortunately, all milk-based beverages are unavailable today."

"What's going on?" Blake asked, walking up to the shop right as Edie was taping the sign to the door.

She tapped the sign in response.

"Well, that's an unfortunate turn of events," Blake said. "I'd estimate that lattes account for no less than 95 percent of our sales."

"It's a real bastard," Edie agreed. "Can you hold down the fort while I go call the customer service line for our espresso machine and see if they can help fix the steamer wand by some miracle?"

"Of course," Blake answered.

The phone call only added to the morning's frustration.

She was instantly greeted with a robot voice asking her why she was calling, and after listening to the lengthy menu of options and hitting 7 for troubleshooting and repairs, she was then prompted to punch in her twelve-digit model number followed by the month and year of purchase. Edie had no idea when her parents had purchased the espresso machine (or even if it *had* been her parents and not her grandparents or great-grandparents) so she then sat on hold for nearly an hour before a human finally answered her call.

"Ma'am, do you have your twelve-digit model number?" the bored-sounding man on the other end of the line asked.

Edie read the number she had found etched in the back of the machine.

"Nothing with that number is coming up in our system."

"It's the steamer part of one of your espresso machines," Edie explained. "It gave a high-pitched squeal and then wheezed itself to death. I need some ideas on how to fix it."

"Ma'am, I really can't help you without the proper model number."

Edie ran a tired hand through her hair and read the model name and number another two more times.

"Are you sure that is one of our units?"

"I pulled this phone number off the side of the machine

right beneath your company's logo." Edie's frustration grew.

There was a long pause and Edie could hear the click of a keyboard from the other side and then finally, "Ma'am, this unit was discontinued over five years ago. I'm sorry, but I will be unable to help you."

"The steamer wand can't be that much different from the newer units. Can't we discuss some troubleshooting options?"

"I'm sorry, ma'am. The only help I can offer you would be to recommend upgrading to one of our newer units."

"Thank you so much," Edie said, her voice dripping with sarcasm as she hung up the phone.

She couldn't afford a new espresso machine. That would only add debt on top of debt. But she also couldn't get by without a milk steamer. Blake was right; lattes accounted for about 95 percent of their business.

"You have had quite the streak of unfortunate luck," Blake said when Edie explained the situation.

Edie pursed her lips and nodded at the very apt statement.

"I have a milk steamer at home that I could bring in," Blake said.

Edie searched his face for any sign that he was bullshitting her, even though Blake was far too serious for practical jokes.

"Would you be willing to donate it?" she asked.

Blake took a moment to consider the question. "I mean, I could bring it in for today, but I don't think I'd want to *donate* it. It was fairly costly."

Edie was desperate. Borrowing a steamer for one day would be like bailing out a sinking ship with only one bucketful of water.

"I can't buy it off of you," Edie said. "If I had the money for that, I wouldn't need to ask you in the first place."

"I could offer you half off the original retail price."

Edie shook her head. She couldn't afford it if he offered her 90 percent off the original retail price.

"What if I traded you my vinyl collection?" Edie offered. "I have all my parents' old records. I could box them up and give them to you. There's over a hundred albums. It would be a fair trade."

Blake considered the offer and then nodded. "You've got yourself a deal."

Edie felt herself exhale some of the stress of the morning. It wasn't a perfect solution, but it was a solution, and it would keep the shop somewhat functional for the moment.

Edie sent Blake home to get his milk steamer, and she held down the shop. She knew that she wasn't going to get her usual break during her split shift, which was when she typically slept. She'd be at the shop all day, from open to close.

Who needs sleep anyway?

She thought about her night with Penny, which already felt like ages ago. She didn't regret getting so little sleep the night before. A day of exhaustion was entirely worth it.

Penny was the one part of her life that wasn't a complete and total disaster.

Red, Red Wine

I'm my own best customer, Edie realized as she poured herself a fourth cup of coffee for the day. What she really wanted was a glass of wine— maybe something stronger— and a good night's sleep.

"You'll bring those vinyl in tomorrow?" Blake asked, as he shrugged into his faux-leather jacket.

"Don't worry, Blake. A deal's a deal." Edie wasn't overly attached to the old records, but the collection was one more loss on top of everything else, and at some point she would still need to replace the broken espresso machine with a more permanent and functional solution.

Blake left for the evening, and Edie tried to brace herself for her solo shift at the coffee shop. She didn't normally mind working the evenings alone, but she was exhausted. Everything with the steamer. . . Then the bank had called to remind her why she *couldn't* buy a new espresso machine because her line of credit was maxed out on the roaster, and they were threatening repossession of the equipment if she couldn't make a payment soon.

The place was circling the drain. She was hemorrhaging

money and time and resources, and it was only a matter of time before the place completely bled out.

Edie finished her coffee and yawned. A quick glance at the clock told her that it was barely past 8:00 p.m. and her whole body sighed in defeat. There was no amount of caffeine that was going to get her through to midnight.

Edie pulled out a piece of paper and a marker, and quickly scribbled the shameful words. For what she believed was only the second time in the shop's history (the first being her parents' funeral) she taped up the sign that read "Sorry. Closed for personal reasons. We'll open again in the morning." Then she tried to stay awake until all the current customers finished their beverages and conversations and the shop gradually emptied.

"I'm sorry, Mom and Dad," Edie said, as she turned the key in the lock. The McLean Family Coffee Shop wouldn't shut down because she'd closed early for one evening, but this small act of giving up felt like the first step toward admitting total defeat and closing the shop for good.

Edie walked the few short blocks back to her apartment. There was an early autumn chill in the night air, and she pulled her jacket tighter around herself. Even the thought of pumpkin spice season and the influx of customers it would bring couldn't lift her spirits. She looked up at the cloudless night sky, and it seemed impossible to her that it was less than twenty-four hours earlier that she'd been looking up at that same sky with Penny, feeling so happy and content.

Edie reached her apartment lethargic and emotionally hungover. She wanted nothing more than to flop onto her bed, close her eyes, and forget that the entire miserable day had ever happened. She could hear the *thump, thump, thump* of bass from her hallway, though, and she knew that sleep would be elusive.

She let herself in and tossed her jacket lazily into a pile by the door, then her gaze lifted, and she froze, realizing the music was coming from the living room, not Empty's bedroom where her roommate typically tended to hibernate.

"Oh, hi," Edie managed, before the details of the sight before her began to settle in. She looked around the room, surprise giving way to confusion, which gave way to concern.

Empty sat in the recliner, with her left sleeve rolled up, while an IV pulled blood from a vein in the bend of her elbow. Dark fluid collected in a blood bag next to her, and Edie quickly noted the yellow latex tourniquet that sat on her end table beside a discarded alcohol wipe and its wrapper. It was a familiar scene, harking back to images of the blood donation drives that Edie had always participated in, except it was happening in her living room while an emo singer belted shrill lines about a thirst for blood. Sid sat casually in her recliner, arms spread wide onto either armrest as though it were a throne, a glass of red wine held loosely in his left hand.

The details of the scene were grotesquely out of place, and yet the most puzzling detail, Edie noted, was the pair of now-familiar gray eyes that had locked on her own. She had spent the previous evening memorizing every detail of those eyes.

"Penny?" she asked in a thin, strangled rasp.

Penny's eyes were wide with alarm or maybe, more accurately, a deer-in-headlights look of guilt.

"Edie." Penny's voice cradled her name with gentle desperation while her hands cradled the bag of Empty's blood.

"I can explain," Empty said.

"No!" The word went off like a gunshot from Penny's mouth.

"It's fine. She's cool," Empty said. "About once a month I donate blood to Obsidian. Penny helps ensure it's all done safely."

44

Except they weren't in a hospital, Penny was wearing a floral blouse and jeans instead of scrubs, and she had a half-empty glass of wine beside her as well.

"Is he sick?" Edie asked.

"Yes," Penny answered, all too quickly.

His pallid skin didn't look unhealthy, just sun starved.

Sid scoffed and took a long, purposeful swig of his wine. "I am the portrait of vitality."

"Please stop." She heard Penny lower her voice and beg.

Edie watched as the blood bag continued to slowly fill, and Penny was forced to turn back to the task at hand, removing the IV and taping a Band-Aid over the injection site.

I think I preferred it when I thought they were track marks.

Empty rolled her sleeve down. Sid smiled around his wineglass before taking another long swallow.

The viscous red liquid sloshed in his glass and stained his lips. A drop ran down the outside of the glass and he caught it with his finger, which he licked clean, and . . .

Oh, God.

It wasn't wine.

Edie's stomach did a violent flip and vomit threatened, but she held it down.

"Drink me in, devour me, drain me,

My vampire king, live on for eternity."

The song lyrics were disgusting in and of themselves, but it began to dawn on Edie just *how* seriously Empty and Sid took their gothic vampire obsession.

More nausea caused her to bend at the waist, and she kept herself propped up with her hands on her knees.

"Edie?" Penny's voice swam to the surface above the waves of nausea. "Can we talk?"

45

"I'll, um, leave you three to do your thing," Edie said, disregarding Penny's question. "Forget I was here."

"Edie," Penny called again, but Edie's sleep-deprived brain felt broken, neurons firing in a million different directions as she tried to process what she'd just walked in on. She wasn't entirely sure she wasn't having some sort of psychotic break or caffeine-overdose hallucination.

Those are a thing, right?

Edie quickly brushed her teeth, changed into a nightshirt, and crawled into bed. When she closed her eyes, visions of the scene in her living room kept replaying in her head.

Empty with the IV pulling blood from her arm . . .

Sid sipping blood from a wineglass while sitting in her recliner like it was a throne . . .

Penny, dressed in such a contradictorily sunny shirt, pulling the IV out of Empty's arm and setting the bag of blood on the end table beside her own half-empty glass of what Edie had initially mistaken for red wine.

Pseudovampiric Blood Kink

Edie stared into the vortex that formed where the steamer wand kissed the surface of the milk with a soft hissing sound.

It was the middle of the night, and she was alone in her coffee shop, having been unable to sleep, overwhelmed with how strange and unfamiliar her apartment now felt. For all of the stress the shop had put her through lately, it was still her happy place, and the place she felt the most connected to both her family and herself.

The gentle frothing of the milk held her in an almost-meditative trance until the metal pitcher became too hot to touch, the short scald of the metal bringing her back to the present. She turned off the machine and poured the milk into the mug she'd set out for herself, already containing the white chocolate powder and lavender syrup, and then she breathed in the soft floral scent of the beverage, missing her parents more than ever.

Lavender white hot chocolate was her favorite feel-good beverage, and not one that her family had ever put on the menu. It was sweet and soothing, and ever since she was a little girl it had been the drink her dad had made for her whenever she was upset. When she'd had a fight with her best friend in elementary school and had come home in tears, he'd made her the hot chocolate. When she'd embarrassed herself by fainting in the seventh-grade school play, he'd made her the hot chocolate, and she'd sipped it while he'd told her his own embarrassing stories to make her feel better. When, at sixteen, she'd nervously told her parents that she was lesbian, both her parents had assured her that they loved her unconditionally and that nothing had changed, and then they'd *all* sat and had the hot chocolate together while her parents had let Edie tell them her truth.

She took a slow sip of the warm beverage, wishing desperately that her parents were with her. Between the debt, the broken steamer, and whatever-the-hell had been happening in her apartment . . . It was all too much, and she had no one to talk to about any of it.

It figures I meet someone who is supportive and kind and sexy and she's into some sort of pseudovampiric blood kink.

She thought of the kiss they'd shared in the bed of the truck beneath the northern lights.

'You smell like sunshine and daffodils, with the lingering scent of coffee clinging to your skin. Like morning on the front porch.'

Had any line ever made Edie melt more?

'You taste like morning, too.'

Then she remembered Penny's lips, stained crimson with her roommate's blood, and her stomach turned.

I can't believe I kissed her.

Maybe it wouldn't have been as bad, had it not all taken place in Edie's apartment, where the memory of her parents was being replaced with occult decor and now a woefully deflated crush.

Maybe it doesn't have to change anything.

48

No. Edie interjected her own thoughts. *I draw the line at blood play.*

She took a sip of her hot chocolate, but couldn't stomach the beverage, so she set it aside and went to the back room to bag beans and count inventory. Anything to distract from the mental replay of the most disgusting social hour she'd ever witnessed.

A knock at the walk-up window interrupted her distraction attempt.

Edie went back out to the main shop, and her stomach twisted itself in all kinds of knots at the sight of Penny, looking so effortlessly attractive in her scrubs, with her hair pulled back loosely, some errant strands framing her face.

It was unfair that she could show up looking that pretty while Edie was sure she looked like a hot mess.

"We *really* don't need to talk," Edie said as she slid the window open.

"We do," Penny argued. "Please. Give me a chance to try to explain."

Edie shook her head, but the pleading look in Penny's eyes chipped away at the wall she'd put up between the two of them.

"Listen," Edie said. "I'm not trying to judge you. To each their own. It's just not a fetish I share."

"Oh my God, is that what you think that was?" Penny asked.

Edie nodded. "Uh, yeah."

"I swear on *everything* that it was nothing sexual."

Edie believed her, but it didn't change the fact that Penny and Sid had been *drinking* Empty's blood. Sexual or not, it made her uncomfortable.

"Can I come in? Sit down and have a conversation?"

"We're opening soon," Edie said. There were rarely customers right off the bat, but Edie wasn't about to mention that, still unsure if she wanted to hear whatever reason or excuse Penny had for what had gone down the other night.

"It doesn't have to be now," Penny said. "I work tonight, but I could come by tomorrow night at closing."

Edie bit the inside of her lip, but the pleading look in Penny's eyes won her over.

"Okay," she agreed.

Penny's smile lit up in the dim light outside the walk-up window. "I'll see you tomorrow night." She gave Edie one last stomach-twisting smile before heading off down the sidewalk, leaving Edie feeling a confusing mix of excitement and fear for whatever it was Penny was going to offer as an explanation.

She busied herself with tedious work until it came time to open the shop for the day, hoping that the work would settle her inner turmoil, but none of the tasks were engaging enough to stop replaying the scene she'd walked in on the other night.

Vampires. She scoffed at the thought of Sid and Empty and their sanguinarian fantasies. The notion that Penny was intertwined in that scene was disconcerting. Penny who had taken her on the most romantic date of her life, who had said the most romantic things, and whose kiss Edie could have drowned in.

She'd been fantasizing about Penny for months, and in one quick moment, that fantasy had burned to ash like a vampire in sunlight.

By the time the coffee shop opened for the day, Edie's sleep deprivation began to catch up to her. She managed to keep her eyes open as she filled orders for the early-morning customers, but she was bone-tired both physically and emotionally by the time she was able to tag out.

"Good morning, Edie," Blake said as he stepped inside to

begin his shift.

Edie snapped instantly awake. "Oh shit."

"You forgot the records." It was a statement, not a question, and it had been spoken with an exasperation that suggested Blake had expected nothing different.

"I'll bring them when I come back this evening for closing shift. I swear."

Blake looked displeased. "I can send you a text reminder."

Edie's irritation simmered into anger. She would never expect Blake to give her his milk steamer for free, but, at the same time, he'd been with the McLean Family Coffee shop for so long, he was practically a member of the McLean family. He could offer her a *little* bit of grace.

"I said I'll bring them," Edie snapped.

Blake recoiled at the uncharacteristic response, and guilt flamed up within Edie.

"Sorry," she said. "I'm in a mood."

"All good." Blake held up his hands in a conciliatory gesture.

Edie turned to head out, but Blake asked, "Does this have to do with coffee take-out girl?"

"What?" Edie spun around so fast she almost knocked over the stack of water cups at the edge of the counter. "Why do you ask that?"

He shrugged. "You've glanced at the walk-up window approximately ten times since I got here."

Edie reddened with embarrassment at how transparent she apparently was.

"I'm going to offer you my two cents," Blake said. "You can do with my advice what you will, but don't date someone who only orders carry-away. Someone who doesn't have the time to sit down for a cup of coffee probably doesn't have the time for much else in their life."

"I'm not— We're . . . nothing," Edie stammered.

Blake gave a disinterested shrug. "I get it. It's lesbian coffee without the coffee."

"This is *not* a lesbian coffee situation," Edie said, regretting ever teaching him that phrase. She and her friends had coined the term "lesbian coffee" to refer to any ambiguous dating situations they found themselves in after Edie had gone on too many coffee dates that she'd not known were dates and had lamented the fact that coffee invitations between lesbians were never clear enough to delineate between a date or a friend invite.

"If you say so," Blake said, and he began wiping down the counters during the lull between customers.

Edie longed for the days when the most she'd had to worry about was how to gently let down the woman who had mistakenly thought they'd been dating for a month.

She should have turned to leave, but instead found herself asking, "Why are vampires so popular?"

"I suppose they make for a relatable allegory," Blake answered.

"An allegory?"

"Who hasn't, at some point, felt taken advantage of, or drained, by someone else." Blake looked at the milk steamer.

"I'll get you your records before you even leave here for the day," Edie said.

Blake shrugged as though he had no idea why Edie might have made that connection.

"Think about vampire lore. They can only come in with permission, and once they're in, they'll suck you dry. Everyone has met a modern vampire. Fiction simply exaggerates real life."

"You've put a lot of thought into this." Edie was surprised

given Blake's disdain for fiction.

"Hardly a fleeting afterthought."

"I still don't get it though," Edie murmured. "How did vampires go from depressing allegory to weird sexual fetish?"

"Oh, yeah, that," Blake said. "That was probably the good-looking actor in that movie."

"Yeah," Edie said, letting the word hang. "That's probably it."

It didn't really matter *why* vampires were so popular or, specifically, what appealed to Penny about them. All that mattered was that she'd gone on a date with someone who was so into vampires that she was literally pretending to *be* one.

There wouldn't be a second date.

Edie had hoped that Empty's late-night vampiric obsession would keep her asleep until noon, allowing Edie the chance to slip into the apartment undetected and go to sleep without ever having to have a conversation. Her hopes were dashed the instant she opened her apartment door and saw Empty piling her things into boxes.

"What are you doing?" Edie asked.

"Um, moving out," Empty stammered. She avoided eye contact with Edie and picked at the lace of her fingerless gloves.

For a moment, the blood-drinking vampire shit was forgotten, and all Edie could think about was the $400 rent that she was going to lose if Empty left.

"You can't move out."

Empty kept piling books into the box on the coffee table.

"Why would you think you have to move out?" Edie asked, placing her arm across the box so that Empty would have to stop putting books inside long enough to talk to her.

"Because I'm 'fucking weird'?" Empty made air quotes with her fingers. "I've heard it before; you don't have to say it. And because I've been kicked out of places for a lot less."

"You're not—" Edie stopped herself because the words would have been disingenuous. "Why though? I mean, I can understand the decor, the clothes, the books and movies, even if none of that's my thing. But literally donating your blood for consumption?"

Empty sighed, and the weariness in that sigh made her look tired far beyond her youth. She took a seat on the sofa, and she no longer looked like the immature, silly girl that Edie had presumed her to be.

"I don't expect you to get it."

Edie didn't want to know the details about Empty and Sid's blood-drinking hobby, so she knew she was going to regret the words, but she spoke them anyway. "Try me."

She watched as Empty warred with herself about what or how much to share.

"Believe it or not, people thought I was pretty fucking weird long before the vampire thing," she said at last. "Obsidian, too."

Edie took a seat on the sofa and waited while Empty gathered her thoughts.

"We met at a summer church camp that our parents sent us to. Obsidian had smuggled in a library copy of *Dracula* and he let me read it when he was done. Our love of vampires took off from there. They made sense to us. Cast out of the church, looking and feeling human, but not *really* being like everyone else . . . We could relate."

The vulnerability in Empty's answer made Edie's breath catch in her chest.

"Anyway, vampires resonated with us, except they're not weak and pitiful like we were. They're strong and feared and immortal."

"And you want to be feared?"

Empty considered the question. "I'm happy with the stories. They're enough for me. But Obsidian, he used to get bullied by the jocks at school. We were openly a couple, but even so, they used to call him a fag because of his skinny jeans and eyeliner. One day, they held him down and wrote the word on his forehead in sharpie. He couldn't scrub it off, and he had to ride the bus home with everyone staring. After that, he wanted to make it real."

Edie's stomach churned. She thought of the cocky way Sid had sat in her apartment, with the glass of—the drink—in his hands, almost confrontational, as though he'd been daring her to say something, and she knew now the vulnerabilities that his bravado hid.

"That's awful," Edie said.

Empty cocked an eyebrow and nodded. "Haven't you ever wanted something to be real badly enough that you were willing to do whatever it takes to make it happen?"

The words hung heavy in the air between them as Edie's thoughts immediately jumped to her coffee shop. She wanted it to survive more than anything. Was that dream filled with just as little reality as Sid's dream of being a vampire?

"Obsidian isn't immortal," Empty continued. "He sunburns more than most, but that's just his Irish ancestry; he won't turn to ash if he steps into the sun. His favorite food is garlic bread, his bat necklace is made of silver, and while it emotionally pains him that his parents make him attend church with them as a condition of living in their basement, he is not physically injured by doing so.

"But we've created a community for ourselves, and the blood drinking legitimizes it for us. It makes it real. It emboldens Obsidian and has created an intimate bond between the two of us. It makes it real *enough*."

"And Penny is a part of that community?" The question slipped out unintentionally, and Edie immediately began to correct herself. "Never mind. I don't want to know."

"I don't know," Empty answered, looking equally puzzled. "I mean, I guess. She participates, but she also seems kind of put-off by our vampire role play."

Edie wasn't sure if that made her feel better or worse.

Empty looked contemplative for a moment, and then she began talking rapidly, possibly more to herself as a way of processing her thoughts than to Edie. "I don't know, she's never said anything, but there's this *look* people tend to give us. The '*you're fucking weird*' look." She looked at Edie. "Yeah, *that* one. Anyway, she gives us that look, like, a *lot*. And I tried talking with her about the latest *Nightfall* novel, and she'd never even heard of the series."

"So, you don't know her all that well then?" Edie asked. It was silly to have felt so relieved by the thought, because while maybe Penny wasn't as deeply involved in the vampire fandom as Empty and Sid, she had still participated.

Empty shook her head.

"There are a few forums for vampire role play in our area. We put out an ad looking for help with the IV and Penny answered. We've tried to ask her about her involvement in the community, but she keeps pretty quiet."

Edie nodded, digesting that information. It raised more questions than answers. Who engaged in a role play community without engaging in the role play?

"Anyway, how do *you* know Penny?" Empty asked.

Edie flashed to an image of Penny just before their kiss, lying against the pillows in the back of her truck, her gray eyes shining nearly silver in the moonlight.

"She's come by the shop a few times," was all Edie offered.

Empty looked like she was going to ask more, and Edie didn't want to talk about Penny so she stood from her chair and said, "Speaking of, I should probably get some sleep so that I'm not bagged when I go in tonight."

"Yeah, of course," Empty said.

"Just . . . don't move out?" Edie couldn't lose the rent money, but more importantly she couldn't stand the thought that Empty would feel like she'd have to leave because of her judgment.

"I won't," Empty agreed. "Thanks for being cool about this."

This was the absolute last thing that Edie wanted to be "cool" about, but she nodded and excused herself.

She wanted to excuse herself from the entire situation.

The Kind of Monster That Turns Down a Good Cup of Coffee

Wannabe-vampires were definitely *not* Edie's type, and yet the evening stretched out painfully slow as her anticipation over meeting with Penny grew with each long, unfulfilling hour.

She supposed that agonizing about the pitiful state of her love life was less threatening than agonizing about the pitiful state of her family's coffee shop. It was a reprieve, at least, from the ever-present dread that she was going to be the McLean family member that let their coffee legacy die.

Business was slow as always. In the far back corner, the crochet club worked on blankets, and since their hands were busy, their drinks went largely untouched. They were one of Edie's favorite groups of regulars, with members ranging from eager preteen to wizened octogenarian, all sharing stories and skills with one another while they worked. But though they stayed for a couple of hours every week, they rarely purchased second beverages or snacks.

Still, Edie took great joy in watching the group work. They embodied everything that Edie had always loved about her family's coffee shop. They were a mismatched group, as colorful a patchwork collective as the granny square blankets that had become so popular among them.

Her family's shop had always been the same: a place where there was a table for everyone. While Jimmies popped up all over the place offering a cheap and fast caffeine fix, her family had always maintained that good coffee made good conversation. It brought people together.

I'm going to miss this.

The thought came to Edie with a sudden, sad pang, and she straightened herself against the feelings of defeat. The McLean Family Coffee Shop wasn't going anywhere.

She was determined. But she wasn't convinced.

As the evening stretched on, customers left with no new customers replacing them until only the crochet club remained, and then even they began to set aside their crochet hooks and pack up their projects. Edie polished the espresso machine and wiped the counter to an almost obsessive-compulsive degree. Anything to breathe life into the stagnant evening.

By the time the clock neared midnight, the shop had been empty for nearly an hour, and by the time the knock finally came from the front door, Edie was fraught with anxiety over the failings in all areas of her life.

She went to the door with knots in her stomach. Even cloaked in the dark of night, the worry lines were visible on Penny's face. She lacked her usual easy confidence, her arms pulling her denim jacket protectively around herself.

The nervousness she saw in Penny tugged at something in Edie, and she softened as she opened the door.

"Invite me in?" Penny asked.

There was something about the way she asked, such a soft,

pleading tone ... Edie couldn't have said no if she wanted to. She stepped back and motioned for Penny to pass her. "Come on in. I'll make us some coffee."

"No need," Penny said as she stepped inside, but Edie went to put on a pot anyway.

Good coffee makes for good conversation. Her dad's words echoed in her mind. But, more than that, making coffee gave her something familiar to latch onto. She didn't know what her conversation with Penny was going to entail exactly, but she knew that it was going to be uncomfortable.

Edie ground just enough beans to make a small pot of pour-over, and she turned on the kettle.

"Come sit and talk," Penny urged.

Edie nodded, but made no move to sit. "I will. Let me just boil the water for our coffee. It'll be worth the wait, I swear."

"Edie, no," Penny said. "It's fine."

Edie fully realized, however, that the act of making coffee was a calming strategy. There was so much uncertainty about how her conversation with Penny was going to go, and she felt so anxious and on edge that she *couldn't* simply stop and sit. She *had* to make the coffee first.

When the water was boiled, she took her time pouring it over the grounds while Penny watched on in silence, and then she took two mugs and the coffee to one of the tables. The same table where they'd repainted the shop sign together, what felt like a lifetime ago.

"Do you take cream or sugar in your coffee?" Edie asked.

"No coffee for me, thanks," Penny said, waving off the beverage.

Edie gave a nervous laugh. "What kind of monster turns down a good cup of coffee?"

Penny blanched a little at the question, and Edie immediately regretted asking it. She'd meant it as a joke, but it clearly hadn't landed that way. It shouldn't have mattered to her whether Penny wanted coffee or not, but she realized she wanted to replace the image of Penny drinking her roommate's blood with the image of the two of them drinking coffee together.

Edie poured herself a mug and took a long, calming sip.

She takes this vampire thing way too seriously, Edie thought to herself. She realized that she'd never seen Penny eat or drink *anything* other than blood, that Penny never entered the shop without being invited in first, and that she only ever saw her after sunset.

"You said you wanted a chance to explain?" Edie began.

Penny looked terrified, but Edie didn't know how to help ease Penny's fears when she felt fear thundering inside herself, as well.

"I really like you," Penny said, taking the conversation in a completely different direction than Edie would have imagined. "Getting to know you lately . . . it's been like sunshine. And you have no idea how long it's been since I've felt that."

"There we go," Edie said. "That's a *weird* thing to say. If you want to read all those vampire novels in your spare time, who am I to judge? You want to pretend to *be* a vampire? That's not my thing, but good for you, I guess. I just . . . have I mentioned it's *really* not my thing?"

"I'm not pretending to be a vampire," Penny argued.

"I know that you were drinking the blood, too," Edie said. "I saw your wineglass the other night, and Empty confirmed it."

Silence echoed between them as Edie waited for Penny to offer a *rational* explanation, like anemia or iron deficiency or something.

Finally, Penny spoke very gently as she said, "Where do you think all of those vampire stories come from?"

"Stephen King? Anne Rice? E.L. Stormbringer?"

"I mean originally," Penny said. "Before all of them. Before Bram Stoker and Dracula. Before any of the fiction. Do you not think that all stories come from *some* place of truth?"

"I've never given it any thought," Edie said. "Blake suggested that vampires emerged as an allegory for something. I don't really know what an allegory is, but that explanation sounds as good as any to me."

"Come on, Edie," Penny begged. "Don't make me say it."

"Say *what?*" Edie's frustration grew.

Penny's eyes were dark with desperation, as she waited for Edie to put the puzzle pieces together, but Edie couldn't land on any real-world explanation.

Finally, Edie blurted out the only thing that came to her mind, as though putting the words out there would let her get past the ridiculous mental block. "It's like you want me to come to the conclusion that the reason you were drinking Empty's blood in my living room the other night is because vampires are real and you're one of them. But that's ridiculous so what are you *really* trying to tell me?"

"Why is it ridiculous?" Hurt was evident across Penny's face, but Edie couldn't process Penny's emotion on top of the bizarre conversation she found herself in.

"What do you mean?" Edie asked. "I just said the world's most outlandish statement and you're not even going to *try* to tell me that I'm way off base?"

Penny offered a pleading gaze but no denial.

Edie reached for her coffee to try to steady her racing thoughts, but her hands shook as she lifted the mug to her lips, and she spilled some on herself. She looked down at the coffee, which was surely going to stain her shirt, and the ludicrousness of the entire night hit her like a wave. The laughter started as a short chuckle, and then it grew until she was wiping tears from her eyes, trying desperately to suck in air while Penny looked at her complete mental break from across the table.

Eventually the laughter subsided, but her heart hammered in her chest and her hands still shook.

"Prove it," Edie said, her voice sounding small and scared. Not that she expected Penny would be able to prove a thing. It wasn't real.

"Take a picture of me," Penny said, sitting still and stoic, unfazed by the request for proof.

"I don't want to take a pic—"

"You want proof?" Penny asked. "Try taking a picture of me."

Edie took her phone out, opened the camera, and snapped a quick photo of Penny sitting across from her.

"There," she said, setting the phone on the table.

"Look at the picture," Penny urged.

Edie sighed, but she picked her phone back up to open her photo gallery. When she saw the photo, she physically recoiled, the legs of her chair screeching across the floor. There was nobody in the photo; the seat across from her was empty.

I'm losing it, Edie thought. *Penny's not sitting across from me. She's a visual hallucination. I'm seeing things.*

But then Penny put her hand on Edie's, and the cold touch shocked Edie back to the present. Without even thinking about it, she slid her chair back a foot, and wrapped her arms protectively around herself.

Penny winced. "I'm not dangerous."

"But you're a . . ." Edie couldn't say the word, so she let the

63

sentence trail off. "You drink blood to stay alive?"

"Only ever ethically sourced blood," Penny said, as though that assurance somehow made everything better. "I would never hurt anyone."

"Ethically sourced blood." Edie rolled the words around on her tongue. They tasted wrong.

"Empty willingly donates her blood. I never asked it of her. I never even *suggested* it to her. The idea came entirely from her and Sid."

"Is Sid . . .?"

"Oh God, no," Penny said, and Edie exhaled a little in relief. "You were right about Empty and Sid being really into vampire role play. It's nothing more than that to the two of them."

"But . . ." Edie tried to form words. She had so many follow-up questions, and she wasn't sure where to start. Her world felt off-kilter, the earth suddenly shifted off its axis. She didn't know how to make sense of the world anymore. "What if Empty *didn't* donate her blood?" she asked eventually.

"Then I'd find blood elsewhere." Penny's answer was matter of fact, as though it would have been no big deal acquiring blood to drink.

"Oh, I'm sure it's that easy," Edie scoffed.

"It's not as hard as you'd think," Penny promised. "I used to get blood from the hospital cast-off. Do you know how much blood is wasted through the blood bank? The shelf life of a blood donation is short—only two weeks. It would be garbage otherwise. I've heard of some vampires occasionally siphoning blood from recent cadavers in the morgue, but from an unwilling, *alive* human donor? Never."

"Vampires," Edie echoed. "Plural."

"Well, yeah," Penny said. "I'm not the only one."

Edie shook her head and pushed her chair back, standing up.

"I need you to leave," she managed, still holding herself protectively.

"Edie—" Penny began, but Edie held up a hand to cut her off.

"I need some time to digest all of this. Please? Give me some time."

Penny looked hurt, but she nodded and walked toward the door.

"Promise me something before I go?" Penny asked, pausing with her hand on the door handle.

"Sure," Edie agreed.

"Please don't tell anyone about any of this."

Edie blinked. She hadn't considered telling anyone, and even if she wanted to, who would she tell that would believe her?

"I probably shouldn't even have told you, but I care about you, and I wanted you to know the truth. I took a big risk in telling you."

"I'm not going to say anything," Edie promised.

Penny's gaze was tender with appreciation as she locked eyes with Edie and said, "Thank you."

Edie felt the words somewhere low inside of her, and she shrugged them off. "Of course."

Penny stepped out into the night, and Edie acutely felt her absence, which was stupid given all that Edie had just learned.

She had bigger concerns than her crush.

Like the fact that she now, apparently, had a massive crush on an honest-to-God *vampire*.

"Can nothing in my life be fucking easy for once?" Edie asked the empty shop.

Pictures of her happier, younger self mocked her from the walls.

"Don't," she said to the photos, and she grabbed her keys to lock up for the night.

But she looked over her shoulder the whole way home.

Fact, Fiction, or Fetish

Edie knew coffee. When she went to her morning shift after learning the truth about Penny, she took solace in the safety that came with her knowledge and expertise. For the few hours she was at work, she relaxed into her very familiar world of roast flavor profiles, perfect microfoam, and latte art. She shut her mind off to the business side of things, which gave her crippling anxiety and self-doubt, and she let herself ease into an almost-reflexive routine.

Then she went home from her shift, and she did what any self-respecting millennial would do when faced with new and unfamiliar information; she turned to Google.

A few years back, vampire mania had blown through the city when E.L. Stormbringer had set the popular *Nightfall* series there, but Edie had bought into neither the craze and the midnight book release frenzy nor the crazy concerns and ensuing book banning. Nothing about that vampire series, or any other vampire story, had ever appealed to her. Not that she expected the fictional series to be a great source of information, but she didn't even have overhyped pop culture as a jumping off point for understanding her new revelations about the world.

Edie didn't know where to start, so she typed *"real vampires"* into the search engine and then took her time combing through the results.

She immediately found ample information on so-called vampire communities of consenting adults, like Empty and Sid, donating blood for one another to consume.

This is a thing?

She clicked open a link that took her to a YouTube documentary and listened as members of these communities showed off their filed teeth and talked about their sanguinarian desires. Many of the individuals interviewed described their thirst for blood as being a legitimate medical need, but while they considered vampirism to be a very real part of their existences, with their day jobs and ability to be captured on camera it was clear their "vampirism" was very different from Penny's, and the documentary provided Edie with no answers or clarity.

The next slew of search results all yielded various attempts to explain vampire lore from a human medical perspective. Edie could have gone her entire life without learning about the *purge fluid* that bodies excrete postmortem, which was attributed to European belief that corpses had reawakened and drank the blood of the living. *Porphyria*, a medical condition that causes skin to blister in sunlight, was offered as an explanation to vampires being unable to exist in the daylight.

Then she read about various historical and cross-cultural variations of the vampire beliefs, dating back all the way from ancient Mesopotamian lore telling the story of a creature named Lamashtu stealing babies from their mothers' breasts and drinking the blood of their fathers to a more modern understanding of vampirism and the discovery of skeletons being unearthed across Europe with teeth removed and large rocks placed in their mouths.

Fear underscored everything she read.

Her search then took her to articles on modern vampire fiction where vampires became romanticized and often represented sex and lust.

One rabbit hole after another.

The problem was, that while the internet was a treasure trove of all things weird and wonderful, there was no way to filter factual information from the fiction or the fetish. Nothing she read made her feel any closer to understanding Penny.

The hours ticked away as Edie clicked through site after site.

She was so absorbed in her search that the rest of the world faded around her, and at the jarring knock at her door she jumped backward, a stack of books falling from the edge of her desk.

"Yeah?" she asked, embarrassment flooding her cheeks as she began straightening her things.

"Um, are you okay?" Empty asked from the other side of the door.

"I'm fine," Edie stammered. "Why?"

"Well, uh, it's 8:00 already, and I don't know, maybe your shop is closed today? But I thought I remember you saying you had a shift tonight."

Edie bolted upright and confirmed the time on her phone. "Shit, shit shit." She scrambled to find her keys on her desk and began mentally running down the list of everything she had to do to get ready.

"I'm coming in," Empty announced, and she pushed open the door just as Edie stood to get ready and was hit with a sudden dizzy spell.

The room spun. Edie grabbed her desk for balance as she

felt for her chair to sit back down.

"Shit," she said again, this time with defeat instead of panic.

Edie's fingers tingled, and she opened and closed her hands into sweaty fists as the spinning gradually slowed.

"Edie?" Empty's eyes were wide with fear.

"I'm fine," Edie promised, though she didn't *feel* fine. "I just need to sit for a minute, and then I'd better get to the shop."

Empty shook her head. "No way," she argued. "You clearly need to stay home and rest tonight. Maybe even go to urgent care to get checked out."

"I don't need to see a doctor," Edie promised. She didn't argue about staying home, though. Empty was right. She'd already more or less missed her shift. There was no point in going in to open the shop only for the closing hours.

"I guess I'm going to make some food," Edie said, but when she tried to stand the dizziness once more overwhelmed her. "Uh, maybe in a few minutes." She sank back into her chair.

Empty looked paler than usual and Edie felt bad for scaring the girl.

"I'm fine," Edie promised. "Maybe just bring me a glass of juice?"

Empty nodded and went to the kitchen, returning quite a while later with a large mug filled with apple juice.

Edie took a sip, the liquid cold on her tongue. "I feel better already," she lied, taking another sip and hoping that the blood sugar boost would cure her dizzy spell. She was certain it was the result of a combination of stress, lack of sleep, and no food, but even that knowledge of a possible cause didn't make it less unsettling as the room spun around her each time she moved to stand.

Edie sipped on the juice slowly, and Empty looked on in

fear, neither of them speaking to one another. And then Edie heard the apartment buzzer.

She didn't have time to question who might be there. Empty quickly said "I'll get it" and rushed from the room.

Edie groaned. She was not feeling well enough to make small talk with Sid.

But a minute later it was Penny who appeared in Edie's doorway, adding insult to injury.

"Hey," Penny said, her voice soft and gentle. "I heard you're not feeling well."

"I'm going to kill Empty," Edie said through gritted teeth, wishing the earth would open up and swallow her whole.

"I was worried about you," Empty said, appearing behind Penny. "I knew you weren't going to agree to go in and checked out, but I figured, Penny's a nurse . . ."

"I wouldn't have consented to this," Edie said.

"That's why I didn't tell you."

"I've got it from here," Penny said to Empty who nodded and was smart enough to know to retreat at that moment.

Penny regarded Edie with a sympathetic gaze.

"I'm fine," she insisted, feeling embarrassment color her cheeks.

Penny moved into Edie's room anyway, crouching in front of Edie and taking Edie's hand in hers, resting two cool fingers over the pulse point in her wrist.

Edie's breath caught in response to the touch, her stomach tightened, and she felt her pulse hit her somewhere decidedly lower, which only added to the embarrassment she felt.

Still, she missed the contact the moment Penny released her wrist.

Penny sat back, and Edie watched in horror as she took in

71

the details of Edie's room.

"It's not always so messy," Edie promised, picking up the notebooks that had scattered on the floor and setting them in a pile on the corner of her desk.

"Have you had anything to eat today?" Penny asked.

Edie grimaced at the question and shook her head.

"How much coffee have you had?"

She considered lying, but there were three empty coffee mugs betraying her on her desk. "I lost count."

"Your heart rate is a bit elevated. You've probably had too much caffeine. And since you haven't had any proper hydration, your blood pressure is probably a little low. Food and sleep will both help."

"I'll get something to eat and then I'll try to sleep," Edie promised, "but as you've noted, I've had a lot of coffee."

Penny gave Edie a look that was part *you're being ridiculous* and part *I really like you*, then said, "Let me make you something to eat."

"I'll just order something," Edie said, but Penny was already heading to the kitchen. Despite feeling lightheaded, Edie stood to follow, sitting as soon as she reached one of the kitchen chairs. "I don't know that I have much."

Penny ignored her and opened the fridge and Edie had to look away as she took in the meager assortment of condiments, milk, and probably expired salad dressing.

Silence stretched between them, and when Edie finally got up the nerve to glance over at Penny, she found her gaping in horror at the pitiful fridge offerings.

"I need to get groceries," Edie said.

"What do you eat?" Penny asked.

Edie didn't want to admit that her diet consisted of heavily processed and fast foods. "There's stuff in my freezer."

Penny pulled open the freezer and frowned down at the packages of frozen TV dinners and chicken strips. "This is it? This is all you have?"

"No," Edie argued. "I also have some ramen packs and microwavable mac and cheese bowls in my cupboard."

Penny shook her head with a look of dismay.

"I want to make you a meal, but there is truly *nothing* for me to work with. When was the last time you had a fresh vegetable?"

Edie didn't have an exact answer, but she knew it was before her parents had died. Since then, she'd been a mess of grief, sleep-deprivation, and debilitating stress.

"Let me order something in."

"Fine," Penny reluctantly agreed. "But I'm coming over with groceries next time, and I'm going to cook you a proper meal."

"Next time," Edie echoed. A slow smile spread across her face. "I like that."

"Somebody has to feed you," Penny teased.

Edie laughed as she pulled out her phone to order some food, but she paused as a thought occurred to her. "I thought you didn't eat food."

"I *used* to," Penny said. "I quite enjoyed cooking before."

Edie quickly ordered herself a donair from her favorite little shop on the corner and then turned back to the conversation. "So how does this vampire thing work?" she asked. "You can't eat food at all?"

"It's complicated."

Penny didn't offer anything else, but Edie patiently waited her out.

"I *can* eat food, but not without blood mixed in. Our digestive systems need blood to function. Eating food without blood would be akin to you sitting down and consuming a bowl of rocks. It would be horrifically painful and dangerous."

"But if you, say, added blood into the tomato sauce, you could eat a pizza?" As soon as the words were out, Edie grimaced at the image.

"Yeah," Penny said. "See your reaction right there? That's pretty much how I feel about it. Some vampires are real foodies, and things like blood sausage and bloody Marys have made their way into human cuisine in modified forms. It's not my thing, though. I need blood to survive, but the thought of adding it into a meal feels like I'm on one of those cooking shows and I've been given the world's worst mystery ingredient. It's not something I *want* to cook with, so I simply don't cook anymore."

Edie thought about her frozen chicken strips and ramen. She felt no passion for food, but she hated the idea of Penny giving up on something she'd previously enjoyed in exchange for mere sustenance.

"Well, I look forward to you cooking for me," Edie said. "Clearly, I could use a proper meal."

Penny laughed and Edie warmed at the little spark of joy that lit up in her eyes. She wanted to see more of that joy.

Her mind flashed back to the memory of lying in Penny's arms in the back of her truck. That night felt like another lifetime, but still, she remembered exactly the way Penny's lips had felt against hers, the way Penny had tasted . . .

"Did you have any other questions?" Penny asked, and Edie was jarred back into the present with all the worries and uncertainties she was feeling.

Edie had questions. Of *course,* she had questions. But she didn't want to go there, so she shook her head.

"Please," Penny urged. "I don't want you having any

misconceptions or lingering fears."

"I don't know what I don't know," Edie said. "I turned on my computer to try to do some research, but each article I read horrified me a little more. I forgot to eat, to sleep, to go to work. I did a deep dive, and I couldn't come up for air."

"Horrified." Penny's shoulders slumped in defeat. "That's a strong word."

"I'm not saying *you're* horrifying," Edie argued. "But the information I found online certainly was."

"That's exactly why I'd rather you come to *me* with your questions."

Shame washed over Edie.

"Do you think that the stuff you read online is true?" Penny asked. Her voice held a defensive challenge, but the note of insecurity was audible underneath.

"I mean, I can't see you gnawing on the bones of babies while washing their flesh down with the blood of their fathers," Edie said, but her joke fell flat.

"I'm not a monster," Penny said. "There's nothing you need to be scared of with me."

Despite Penny's reassurances, Edie's mind played over the centuries of vampire fears and folklore she'd read about. She felt safe with Penny, but the stories had to have come from somewhere.

"People have always feared what they don't understand," Penny said, as if reading Edie's thoughts. "Any holes in human understanding got filled in with make-believe. Stories were spun about us, and those stories were *meant* to be scary. The fear of our differences was used to isolate and control us."

Edie sat back and tried to digest everything Penny was saying.

"Vampirism is 'unnatural.'" Penny made air quotes with her fingers. "We're 'predators.' We represent 'lust,' and 'sin,' and 'corruption' as we turn the honest and faithful to our devious lifestyle. Sound familiar?"

Edie understood the parallel Penny was trying to draw, and discomfort welled within her. It was different, wasn't it? Queerness and vampirism?

"Vampires need human blood to survive," Edie said. "I want to believe that the stories are all borne out of fear, but can you really tell me that vampires have *never* killed people to satisfy that need?"

Penny's eyes held a storm of emotion: anger, injustice, defiance, and defeat.

"Can you tell me that *people* have never killed people?" Penny asked at last.

The answer was the opposite of what Edie had wanted to hear, only confirming her fears. "It's different," she protested.

"Is it?" Penny asked. "Wars, slavery, the holocaust . . . There's no shortage of monstrous deeds that people have committed upon one another. I can't say that no vampires have ever killed anyone, but we aren't a monolith any more than people are. Humans have shown themselves to be just as bloodthirsty."

Edie blew out a breath as she struggled to fully digest everything Penny was saying.

"We're biologically different," Penny argued. "Not morally."

Conflicting emotions warred within Edie. On the one hand, it was petrifying to think that vampires, immortal creatures that survived indefinitely by drinking the blood of humans, existed. On the other hand, this was Penny who'd been visiting her shop for months to buy coffee for all her coworkers, Penny who had helped her repaint her family's worn-down coffee shop sign,

Penny who'd driven her out to the dark sky preserve and whose arms she'd fallen asleep in after kissing beneath the northern lights. Vampires terrified her, but with Penny she felt entirely safe, and she struggled to integrate the two vastly different feelings.

She wasn't sure what to say, but she didn't want the tension she felt between herself and Penny, nor did she want Penny thinking she was afraid of her, so she took Penny's hands in hers and traced her thumbs over the backs of Penny's palms. She felt Penny relax into the touch.

A knock at the door saved her from having to put reassurance into words she didn't yet have.

"My donair." Edie started to get up, but Penny motioned for her to remain seated.

"I'll get it for you. You keep resting."

She returned a moment later with a small plastic bag containing a hot sandwich wrapped in foil.

When the smell of food hit her, Edie realized how ravenous she was, and she dove into the donair while Penny watched on in amusement.

She was too hungry for embarrassment.

As the sandwich settled into her stomach, she noticed that the edge of her anxiety had eased. She no longer felt shaky, and her thoughts cleared.

"Sorry," Edie said as she finally slowed to enjoy the last half of her sandwich. "Is there an anxious counterpart to '*hanger*'? Hanxious? I think I just needed food."

Penny didn't laugh at her attempted joke. "You probably needed something in your stomach to absorb all that caffeine. Food and sleep are what you need."

Edie finished her meal and crumpled the wrapper, placing it

back in its plastic bag to toss in the trash.

"Now you're going to get some rest," Penny said.

Edie opened her mouth to protest, but Penny held up a hand. "You can't keep burning the candle at both ends. Get some sleep. Morning will come soon."

With that, Penny gave Edie a soft kiss on the forehead and let herself out of the apartment.

Despite herself, Edie yawned. She didn't want to sleep. She still had a lot to think and read about. But she crawled into bed anyway, and when her head hit the pillow, she realized just how tired she was.

(Un)Screwed

Dungeons and Dragons night always brought a lively energy to the coffee shop, which helped counter some of Edie's exhaustion. She smiled as she watched the group set up in their usual corner.

The dungeon master, a petite blond girl with a pink streak in her hair, sat behind her screen quietly sipping tea, but when battles occurred, she role-played the monsters with gusto, never seeming to care if all heads in the shop turned to watch her.

One of the players, a lanky young man with sandy hair and thick glasses, had a very obvious crush on her, though she seemed not to realize as much. The man was wiry and looked like he might blow over in a strong wind, but he role-played that he was a strong and charismatic paladin, out saving the world. He gave the role his all each week, and Edie suspected he hoped their dungeon master would come to see him as his character.

Somehow, there was also a man a good decade older who'd come to be in the group, despite having little in common with the other players. He found a way to mansplain nearly everything, from coffee, to game rules, to random social issues. Edie would have found it hard to spend more than an hour with him, but his group seemed to embrace his social quirks and his play style, which was to simply behead everything in his way.

They'd even wholeheartedly welcomed their newest member, the man from the writing group whom Edie had suggested run his plot problems past the D&D band. He had decided to join the campaign, and they indulged the fact that his character was very clearly taken from his book and that he often tried to sneak plot questions into the game night.

Edie admired the welcoming nature of the group. While she aspired to be equally welcoming and nonjudgmental, she was realizing how many snap judgments she made. She'd judged Empty and Sid off the bat based on their chosen names and personal aesthetics, and while some of her assumptions about them hadn't been far off (they *did* practical consensual blood consumption, after all), when she'd learned a bit of their histories, she was able to expand her understanding of them. She'd judged Penny, too. When she'd first met Penny, her infatuation was based on positive assumptions, and then when she'd seen Penny with Empty and Sid, her assumptions had swung in the opposite direction.

"This is why I can't be traveling with an orc!" The writer who'd joined the D&D group stood to emphasize the proclamation.

The older man who always had something to say simply sat back and smirked. "I could behead you next."

"If you behead him, then we don't have anyone to speak elvish when we enter the high castle, so how are we supposed to negotiate the release of our hostages?" The young paladin then turned to face his other teammate. "And it's easy to judge him for beheading everyone, but you weren't complaining five minutes ago when he beheaded the goblin that was about to shoot you in the back with an arrow."

Both of the other players looked appropriately chastised.

"We're stronger together *because* of our differences."

It was cheesy pat advice, but it was evidently what both players needed to hear because they once again began collaborating on their mission. And it was evidently what Edie needed to hear because her mind instantly went to Penny. She was struggling to embrace vampirism, but maybe she needed to stop focusing so much on *what* Penny was and focus more on *who* she was— something that couldn't be learned through a Google search.

It wasn't exactly coincidence that Penny stepped up to the walk out window at that moment right behind one other customer—Edie had been thinking about Penny most of the night—but it still felt a little serendipitous, and Edie greeted Penny with a warm smile.

The woman ahead of Penny ordered a latte, and Edie hurried to fulfill the order. Blake's hand steamer was finicky at the best of times, and in Edie's distraction, she caused a spray of milk, which she quickly wiped up with embarrassment as both Penny and the other customer looked on.

"Sorry," Edie said, after she'd remade the steamed milk to add to the espresso and was able to hand the woman her latte.

Penny chuckled as she stepped forward. "Why are you using that thing?"

"I'll have you know, that fine piece of equipment is one of the most expensive items here," Edie said. "It cost me my parents' vintage record collection, which was surely worth much more than this."

"So it's a prized possession," Penny summarized, "but why?"

Edie sighed as she recounted her tale of woe. "The steamer broke on my espresso machine and because the machine is basically as old as the shop itself, customer service was unable to assist. I also cannot afford a new espresso machine."

Penny looked on with a mix of sympathy and amusement.

"It's not funny," Edie said. "This thing sucks."

"You know," Penny said, "I could probably help you fix the espresso machine."

Edie rolled her eyes. "Yeah right. That thing's a dinosaur."

Penny shrugged. "I'm actually kind of handy."

When Edie realized the seriousness of the offer, she sobered. "You're going to fix my steamer wand?"

"I'm going to try," Penny amended. "I'll come by after my shift, before you open in the morning.

Apprehension tugged at Edie, but she couldn't come up with an argument against trying. "Why not?" she agreed. "What's the worst that could happen?"

Nine hours later, however, as Penny unplugged the espresso machine, setting it face down in front of her, Edie found herself answering that question with all kinds of worst-case-scenarios . . . all of which left her with no way of making espresso at her coffee shop.

"Do you have a tool kit?" Penny asked.

Edie went to the back room to get the small tool kit that had seen more use in the past couple months than it had previously in her entire lifetime. When she'd taken it out to repair her shop sign, it had been covered in a thick layer of dust. The McLean family were not handy folk.

Penny went through the tool kit. She set a screwdriver on the counter but frowned as she couldn't find whatever else she was looking for.

"Do you have a set of needle-nose pliers?" Penny asked.

"I don't even know what needle-nose pliers are," Edie answered.

Penny rolled her eyes with a smile and shook her head, but

it didn't appear to be too much of a problem because, before Edie could ask another question, Penny was pulling the espresso machine over toward the edge of the counter, and she was unscrewing all the tiny screws from the back casing.

Edie watched on in horror as her entire espresso machine was systematically deconstructed.

"I hope you know what you're doing."

"I'm opening it up to check the pump and all the connections," Penny said. She sounded confident, as though the screws scattered across the counter didn't look like tiny corpses of all of Edie's hopes and dreams.

"Okay, I'll accept your vampirism," Edie said. "I'm not scared that you're going to drink all my blood or whatever. But I am *terrified* of you right now for other, far scarier, reasons. You know that this is not only my livelihood, but my family's pride and joy and legacy, right? You know that *four generations* of the McLean Family dreams are all riding on me? Please say you understand how much is riding on this machine still making espresso when you're done."

Penny chuckled as though Edie was being needlessly melodramatic, and she pulled at the back metal panel (far too hard in Edie's opinion) in an attempt to get it free.

The panel didn't come off.

"*Fuck*," Penny muttered under her breath, and this time Edie's terror edged closer to panic.

"What's wrong? Please tell me nothing's wrong."

"Would you like to wait outside?" Penny asked.

Edie shook her head and sealed her lips together, though she couldn't promise how long she'd stand quietly by as Penny massacred her baby.

Penny gave another hard tug and then once again swore

beneath her breath. "There has to be another screw here somewhere."

"You know what? We can just close it up." Edie had managed less than a minute of silence. "I can keep using Blake's steamer until I can afford to replace this thing. It's bound to happen sometime in the next fifty years, right?"

"I've got this," Penny said, and she thoroughly examined the machine, tilting it upside down and sideways, before she finally said "aha," and began removing one final screw from the back panel, which then popped off with ease. No hard pulling necessary.

The inside of the machine was scarier than any horror movie monster Edie had ever seen, with a tangle of various colored wires, tubes, and gears.

Penny, however, did not seem intimidated, and she began disconnecting wires, pushing them to the side. She disconnected tubes, removed a few screws, and then easily lifted out one large gear box, with pipes sticking out. From where Edie stood, it looked as though Penny had removed the heart of the beast.

Edie had to close her eyes as Penny tinkered with the pump. When she dared look again, Penny was placing it back in the open chest cavity of the espresso machine and closing it all back up.

"Let's give this a try," Penny said, as she put all the screws back into place.

Edie felt as though she had just watched Penny perform major cardiac surgery and she was very aware of the thundering of her own heart in her chest.

Once the screws were back in place, Penny plugged in the machine and turned it on. It sounded healthier already.

"All right," Penny said, "how do we do this?"

Edie stepped forward, her hands shaking as she turned the dial. When water began to hiss from the wand, and then the pump began steadily pumping steam, Edie's knees almost buckled with relief.

"It works," Penny said, tossing her hands in the air.

"I don't know if I've ever been more attracted to anyone," Edie said.

"It wasn't that difficult."

Edie turned the steam wand off, though she was tempted to turn it back on just to be sure if *really* was fixed.

"How did you learn to do that?" Edie asked,

Penny shrugged. "I've always enjoyed working with my hands, and I've had a good number of years to perfect some skills."

Edie flushed as her mind instantly took her to thoughts of what other things Penny's hands might be particularly adept at.

"You're really sexy, you know that?" Edie said before she could filter the words.

Penny laughed, but Edie held her gaze.

"I mean it," she said.

She watched emotion play across Penny's face, namely a relief that appeared as big as the relief Edie had felt a moment earlier. Edie realized it was the first easy interaction they'd had since their night at the dark sky preserve. The first moment they'd been able to just be Penny and Edie again.

Edie didn't let any more thoughts overwhelm her. She closed the distance, pressing her lips to Penny's, tentative and gentle.

But it didn't take long before Penny responded, leaning into the kiss and deepening it with an intensity that caused Edie's heart to quicken its pulse. Penny pressed Edie against the counter, and Edie was aware of every inch of their bodies pressed against one another.

"But, just as quickly as the kiss flared into searing intensity, Penny stepped back, placing one final peck on Edie's lips.

Edie tried to pull Penny back to her, but Penny shook her head and indicated toward the door.

"I have to get going," Penny said.

"Just a few more minutes," Edie begged, trying to pull Penny back into the searing kiss for just a little while longer.

"I wish I could," Penny said. "But the sun is going to be coming up soon."

Edie frowned, but she looked out the window and couldn't argue with Penny. A thin line of sun was visible just on the horizon. If Penny was hoping to avoid the burn of the sun, she was going to have to get going.

"Thank you for your help tonight," Edie said.

Penny smiled—a sexy, confident smile. "I told you I wouldn't break it," she said, and she stepped out into the night.

Draculatte!

The morning rush went a *lot* smoother with Edie's steamer wand working once more, and for the first time in months, Edie felt as if something was going right with her coffee shop. It was a small win, but that little victory instilled an infinite amount of hope. It was the confidence boost she needed.

Of course, she had Penny to thank for that victory. Somehow, she and Penny had found their lives inexplicably intertwined. When she'd first met Penny, she had felt an almost indescribable pull. There had been an instant connection, and Edie had looked forward to the few minutes they'd share each night at the window when Penny came by to order the coffees to take to her coworkers. She hadn't known Penny's name, so she'd assumed the connection was nothing more than infatuation, but the more time she spent with Penny, the deeper that connection went.

And of all the people in the city, what were the odds that Edie would find Empty to be her roommate, and Penny would find Empty to be her willing blood donor. Sure, there probably weren't that many people in the city willing to donate their blood for consumption, so that second population pool was likely rather small, but it still seemed like an incredible coincidence that their lives had come together in the way that they had.

If Edie had found a different roommate . . .

If Penny had found a different way of obtaining blood . . .

If Edie hadn't gone home from work that night, exhausted . . .

"Do you believe in soul mates?" Edie asked Blake as they worked together to fill customer orders.

"Absolutely I do," Blake said.

"Really?" His response shocked Edie, who had fully expected him to give her a long lecture against such magical thinking.

"I've been reading Jung's work," Blake said, "and I'm fascinated with his writings on the soul, the unconscious, and coincidence. I absolutely believe that people can connect on a level that transcends the physical lived experience."

Edie turned on her working steamer and sighed as her mind flashed to Penny fixing the machine for her. Penny who was incredibly good with her hands . . .

She had needed Blake to provide her with a reality check, but instead her dreamy thoughts about Penny only intensified.

After the morning rush died down Edie pulled out her notebook and took a seat at one of the tables, deciding to use the remainder of the morning shift to brainstorm some ways she could generate income while she waited for more customers to filter in.

She opened the notebook to a blank page and drew a bunch of dots down the side for the bullet points she didn't yet know how to fill in. Then she tapped her pen on the table as she tried to think of some things that might help.

"Pumpkin spice marketing campaign," she wrote next to the first bullet point. She knew the idea was beyond weak. Besides being overdone at every coffee shop in the city, it was already almost October and so pumpkin spice season was already half over.

"Latte art lessons." She immediately vetoed that idea. For every registration fee she'd lose at least triple as people started making their coffees at home.

"Speed dating." She shook her head as she wrote the idea. Nothing about her dated coffee shop gave off romantic or sexy vibes. Yet another reason it seemed a small miracle that she and Penny had found each other there.

Edie sighed. Like a teenager, she wrote her name on the top of the page and then drew a little heart around it.

God, it was so silly to be smitten with a vampire. And yet her feelings for Penny felt like the most natural thing in the world.

Focus! She shook her head and looked back down at her mostly empty list, still daydreaming about Penny and vampires and how amazing it all was, all the while trying to think of something, anything, she could do as a marketing push for her coffee shop, and all of a sudden, an idea began to take root in her mind.

"It's almost Halloween," Edie said. She hadn't meant to speak the words out loud, but the excitement had caused the words to bubble right out of her.

"It is," Blake agreed, looking over at Edie with confusion and concern etched across his face.

Edie tapped her pen on the notebook a few times as she let the idea percolate for a moment. "What if we lean into that" she asked. "Forget fall flavors and pumpkin everything. What if we ran a Halloween special instead of a fall special?"

"I assume you have an idea in mind?" Blake asked, and she could hear the wary skepticism laced into this question.

But Edie did have an idea, and she could feel in her bones that it was a good one. After everything that had happened, it felt right. It felt as though she'd been guided to the idea by external forces that had brought everything together so perfectly for her.

"What about a Halloween drink?" Edie proposed. "I was thinking maybe something vampire themed."

The name hit her with such a sudden clarity that Edie *had* to believe the inspiration was more than a mere stroke of imagination.

"We can call it a Draculatte!"

Blake groaned.

"What's that about?" Edie asked, feeling her spirits dampen.

"Well, first off, it's such a gimmicky idea," Blake said. "It's so commercial."

"And that's a bad thing?" Edie asked. "I thought that was the point."

"I mean, sure," Blake said. "If you want to let go of integrity in exchange for money."

"That's actually exactly what I want," Edie confirmed, thinking about the most recent call from the bank she'd received.

"It's also likely to cause a bit of a stir," Blake said. "All of the *Nightfall* nonsense has finally calmed down."

Edie had been in Peru during the last book's release, but she'd heard how the books had brought an influx of occulty tourism to town, which had largely gone over very poorly. The books had been banned from all bookstores and libraries in the city. Schools had forbidden talk of the books. The vampire series was called out for its lustful, liberal, very queer undercurrents.

"A little controversy could help our cause," Edie said. At the end of the day, it was nothing more than a punny drink name, so she couldn't see it going over too terribly, and maybe a little fire behind that punny drink name could be the spark her shop needed to get people flocking in the doors.

"It's just for Halloween," Edie promised.

Blake frowned but begrudgingly agreed that the drink's name was clever, and that maybe it had a certain degree of "commercial marketability,"—words that appeared physically painful for him to say but were music to Edie's ears.

She turned to a new page in her notebook and began jotting down ideas in a fevered scrawl. It would be a raspberry oat latte, and on top she'd put whipped cream with two bite-mark raspberry syrup drops on top. Besides being punny and seasonal, Edie wanted to ensure that the drink was aesthetically pleasing so that it would show well on Instagram. She needed social media to start doing more for her, and creating a pleasing looking drink was the one way she knew how.

The more she thought and planned through the idea, the more excited she was about it. She could roll it out the following Monday, giving her nearly a week to do a few mysterious social media posts promising that something new would be coming soon. All five of her followers could get excited. She hoped that word would spread, and she'd be able to maybe build some buzz.

Draculatte! Edie smiled to herself at the idea.

It was going to sell coffee.

As excited as Edie was about her vampire-inspired latte marketing plan, it wasn't something she wanted to blurt to Penny through the walk-up window at work, which, while they both worked long hours for a few nights, was the only way they were able to see one another. And it was so not enough.

Settle down, Edie tried to remind herself. *You hardly even know this girl.* And yet, the connection felt deeper than one date and a handful of encounters should have warranted. Penny had trusted her with a pretty big personal revelation. That meant something, right?

It was irrelevant whether or not her feelings were developing at an appropriate pace, because either way she gave a happy little sigh when she saw Penny swing by to pick up the coffees for her coworkers on her way to work.

"Hi, you," Penny said, leaning with one arm against the window.

Edie felt herself blush, and her embarrassment at that fact resulted in further blushing.

"Hi yourself," Edie managed. "What can I get you tonight?"

She took Penny's order and filled the tray of coffee mugs with coffee, setting the little cream pods and sugar packets in the center of the tray. As she handed the tray through the window, both she and Penny spoke at the same time.

"When can I see you again?"

"When's your next night off?"

They both laughed and Penny tipped her hand to Edie to allow her to answer.

"The shop is closed Sundays," Edie said.

"Perfect," Penny answered. "I was thinking that I could come by and make that dinner I promised you?"

A little electric shock of joy surged through Edie. It would be the perfect time to tell Penny about her Draculatte idea and talk through the marketing plan, but, even better, they could spend some actual quality one-on-one time together. Something Edie had all sorts of thoughts about.

"I can't wait," Edie said.

"Neither can I." Penny held Edie's gaze for a long moment, before reluctantly looking down at her watch. "I do have to run, though. I overslept this evening."

"We'll talk soon," Edie said and waved a little goodbye, her gaze trailing after Penny as she took off down the street.

"That girl gives you quite the dopamine boost," Blake said, nudging Edie with his elbow as he walked past her.

"What?" Edie asked.

"It's the pleasure chemical in our brains," Blake said. "Your brain is practically overflowing with it after talking to her."

"When you put it like that, it sounds so dry and unromantic."

"I mean, attraction is pretty much basic biochemistry," Blake argued.

"What about the conversation we had earlier about soul mates?" Edie asked. Not that she'd necessarily categorize Penny in such a strong term. It was far too soon for that, but she preferred to think that her connection with Penny was on a deeper level than a simple neurochemical reaction.

"Oh, I absolutely believe in soul mates," Blake said. "I also think they're really rare and that most likely you're just feeling a mix of arousal and dopamine."

"That's a sexy thought, Blake," Edie said. "Thanks."

"You're welcome," Blake said, as though not recognizing Edie's sarcasm. "Enjoy your pleasure chemicals."

Edie rolled her eyes, but she was still smiling. She *was* enjoying it, and even if Blake didn't see it, she knew that her relationship with Penny was made of more than pleasure chemicals.

Blood Red Bisque

A date with Penny had sounded wonderful until Edie woke up on Sunday morning and took in the state of her apartment, realizing it was far from presentable. Which, if there was a silver lining, meant that she spent the day leading up to the date stressing about her apartment instead of the date itself. She was so focused on making sure all of Sid's cereal bowls were washed and put away, and that the living room was decluttered of all Empty's occult paraphernalia, that the hours flew by.

It didn't matter that Penny had seen her place before. If she was going to have Penny over on a real date, she wanted to show what her home would look like, rather than its new normal state of unfamiliar goth lair.

When everything was cleaned to her satisfaction, she lit a few scented candles (her candles that were scented of honey and lavender, and not Empty's candles that had names like "bat blood" and "witch hazel," which she hid in the hall closet) and then she went to get dressed for the evening, opting for skinny jeans and a sweater, with a touch of makeup to elevate the casual clothing.

Then there was nothing to do but wait.

Edie went back out to the main living space and found Empty at the kitchen table.

"Don't worry, I'll be out right away," Empty promised. "Sid and I are going to the movies. I'm just waiting for him to pick me up."

Edie looked at the instant coffee container, which had been left open on the counter surrounded by grounds, as well as the mixing spoon next to it. The bread had also been left open on the counter, with crumbs and a greasy butter knife sitting next to the toaster. Irritation threatened to dampen her spirits, but she tamped it down, wanting to feel nothing but excitement for the evening ahead.

Edie cleaned the counter while Empty ate her toast, and then she heard Empty's phone ping.

"That's my cue. Enjoy your evening," Empty said, and she went to the door, leaving her plate and toast crusts on the table behind her.

"Have you seen my keys?" Empty asked, coming back and moving things around on the counter before Edie could stop her.

"I hung them on the key ring beside the door," Edie said, the irritation quickly bubbling up.

"We have a key ring?" Empty asked, but she went to the door and took her keys. She waved a final goodbye and headed out to meet Sid.

Edie glanced at the clock. She didn't know exactly what time Penny would be there—she'd said she was going to go for groceries once the sun set and then she'd be there— but she knew she didn't have *much* time left as the sun had set at least an hour earlier. She quickly set to work putting Empty's dishes into the dishwasher; wiping crumbs from the counter and the table; and putting things back into cupboards, the fridge, and the pantry. She put the lid on the container of instant coffee and considered tossing the insulting caffeinated powder straight into the garbage. She'd have to have a talk with Empty about that later.

Instead, she tucked it at the very back of the cupboard, and then she heard her buzzer.

"Come on up," Edie said into the intercom, and she unlocked the front door to the apartment so that Penny could come in.

She opened the door and watched for Penny to round the corner to her hallway, noting the silly smile on her face the moment she saw her, carrying a large reusable grocery bag that looked heavy, though she carried it effortlessly.

"You look nice," Penny said.

"Thanks," Edie said, feeling her cheeks redden. "So do you." Penny was wearing black jeans with a flowery collared shirt buttoned down the front, which she'd tucked into the waistband of her jeans. Gray boots elevated her a further inch above their already slight height gap.

"Come on in," Edie said, stepping to the side and holding the door for Penny.

Penny smelled like vanilla, and Edie breathed in the soft scent as she brushed past and walked to the kitchen to set down the groceries.

"What's on the menu for tonight?" Edie asked.

Penny began pulling groceries out of the bag. "I was thinking tomato soup and focaccia."

"Like, from *scratch* tomato soup?" Edie asked, eyeing the tomatoes that sat on her counter. She'd never made soup that hadn't come out of a can or a ramen packet.

Penny nodded as though it was no big deal. "I guess

technically it'll be a tomato *bisque.*"

Edie laughed. "Ooh, fancy."

"I promise you it sounds fancier than it is," Penny said. "It's actually very simple."

Edie doubted that was true, but she didn't question it.

Penny took a moment to familiarize herself with Edie's kitchen, and then she turned on the oven and pulled out a sheet pan.

"Can I help you with anything?" Edie asked.

Penny shook her head. "No, you cannot. You're going to sit there and let me take care of things tonight."

Edie liked the take-charge tone in Penny's voice, and she realized she couldn't remember the last time she'd been able to sit back and let others take care of anything. Everything rested on her shoulders these days. It felt unnatural to hand over control, but she took a seat on one of her stools and rested her elbows on the counter to watch Penny work.

Penny washed the tomatoes and laid them out on the roasting pan, as well as a red bell pepper and an onion that she quartered. Then, she covered the vegetables with a generous drizzle of olive oil, as well as salt, pepper, and oregano. All of which she pulled out of her grocery bag, which was good, because if she'd been hoping that Edie had any kitchen staples, she'd have been sorely mistaken. She might have had a salt shaker, but she couldn't even promise that.

Penny popped the tray into the oven and went back to the counter where she pulled a bottle of white wine out of her grocery bag.

"You've come with everything," Edie commented.

"You deserve a proper meal," Penny said. She held out the bottle. "Would you care for a glass?"

Edie didn't drink often, and she'd been running on fumes for so long that she was fairly certain more than one glass would knock her out, but the bottle was chilled and dripped with condensation. It looked cold and inviting, and she had a pretty girl in her kitchen offering it to her, so she nodded.

"Just one glass, though. Otherwise, I might be unconscious for the rest of the evening."

Penny expertly uncorked the bottle, then went to Edie's cupboard for a wineglass and poured a small glass.

The perfect amount.

Then she pulled out the next stool, slid it right next to Edie and took a seat, so close their legs were touching.

Edie took a long, slow sip of the wine as if it might calm her the sudden jolt of nerves she was experiencing.

"Now, we wait," Penny said.

"That's it?" Edie asked.

"For now. There will be a little more work toward the end, but it truly is the easiest dinner ever."

"Dang," Edie replied. "All this time, I thought I had to put up with the canned crap because real soup would be too difficult."

"Now you have no excuses."

Edie laughed and took another sip of her wine.

"It's nice to see you laugh," Penny said.

Edie felt the lightness in her limbs. Such a welcome reprieve. She was under a near constant weight of grief and pressure. Losing her parents, trying to keep the coffee shop afloat . . . She was being crushed by it all.

Except when she was with Penny. Any moments of happiness over the past few months had been with her.

Edie angled her body toward her and leaned forward, resting her hands on Penny's knees and capturing her lips with her own.

Penny took in a small, surprised gasp of air, and then sank into the kiss, her lips soft and yielding, cool fingers tracing over Edie's jaw.

The kiss was tender and sweet, but when Edie pulled back, it was with the hope that there would be more to come, and she saw that desire mirrored in the depths of Penny's eyes. She left one hand resting on Penny's knee.

"What was that for?" Penny asked.

Edie shrugged. "Maybe I like you a little."

"Is that so?" Penny's eyes sparkled.

Edie held her thumb and forefinger close together. "Like, a little."

"Well, I like you, too," Penny said. "More than a little."

The words and the seriousness with which they were spoken made Edie's stomach tighten, and her heart beat a little quicker.

"So . . ." Edie began, trying to choose exactly the right words. "I was thinking about you the other day, and an idea came to me. I was wanting to run it past you."

"Tell me more," Penny said, her voice flirty. Edie had to push aside the other ideas that came to her mind so she could properly pitch her Draculatte plan.

"First of all," Edie began, "I want you to know that this is in no way trying to reduce your identity to any kind of trite pop-culture reference. This is really only meant to be a fun, Halloween marketing idea."

"You're worrying me," Penny said, sitting back and narrowing her eyes at Edie.

Edie took a breath to steady her nerves.

"Halloween is coming up, and I had vampires on the brain, and I thought that maybe a fun marketing plan that could help bring in some revenue would be to market these."

Edie pulled up the little social media infographic that she'd made on her phone. It said, "Try our seasonal Draculatte!" with a picture of a latte covered in whipped cream with twin blood drops made with raspberry syrup on top.

"I think it's a fun idea," Penny said. "Very marketable. I hope you sell lots of them."

Edie didn't realize just how nervous she'd been for the pitch until she heard the genuine positive reception in Penny's voice.

"You're really okay with it?" Edie asked.

"Of course," Penny said. "As previously mentioned, I like you. I want to see your coffee shop succeed. If I can tangentially inspire something that will help your shop, then I'm happy about that."

Edie's cheeks hurt from how wide she was smiling. "I really think it is a fun idea. Something to make my little coffee shop stand out for the month of October, at least. It's not going to single-handedly save the place, but I think it could make a real difference."

Penny laughed. "I like seeing this enthusiasm. Let me know if I can help in any way."

"I will," Edie promised.

Before Edie could say anything else, Penny got up and opened the oven to check on the roasting tomatoes. The smell hit Edie like a wave and her stomach growled desperately in response.

"Oh my God, that smells amazing," Edie said.

"I told you; this meal couldn't be easier."

Penny went to her bag on the counter and pulled out a pan full of dough, sprinkled with various herbs.

"The bread is from scratch, too?" Edie asked.

"Also, not that hard," Penny promised, though Edie didn't

believe her for a second. "It's four ingredients. I mixed them together yesterday to give the dough plenty of time to rise. All that's left to do is pop this in the oven once the veggies come out."

"Now you're just showing off," Edie said.

Penny tossed her a grin that hit her warm and low. "Maybe I want to impress you a little."

Penny then went through Edie's cupboards until she found a large pot, which she set on the stove. She pulled the vegetables out of the oven and scraped all the deliciously charred veggies into the pot. She then followed the contents of the pan with some veggie stock and switched her pan of bread into the oven.

Edie watched Penny as she worked with an almost-choreographed rhythm.

Soon the smell of fresh baked bread joined the savory aroma of the soup, and Edie's hunger accelerated.

While in reality the meal came together quite quickly from there, it *felt* like an eternity before Penny used the immersion blender that she'd brought to blend the contents of the soup before finally ladling it into a bowl for Edie.

Her stomach ached with need by the time the bowl of soup and small plate of bread were set in front of her.

She dipped her spoon into the blood-red bisque. A drizzle of olive oil and dusting of fresh cracked black pepper sat on the surface, and Edie gave it all a stir, before blowing on a spoonful and bringing the soup to her lips.

Her eyes closed as the exquisite flavor hit her. It was easily one of the best things she'd ever eaten.

She then picked up the focaccia and took a bite of it on its own, moaning at the rich flavor that exploded in her mouth, before using the bread to sop up the soup.

It wasn't until she'd taken a number of hungry spoonfuls of soup that she slowed and noticed Penny watching her with a satisfied grin.

"It's weird having you watch me eat," Edie noted.

"Sorry," Penny said.

Edie looked down at her soup and stirred it with her spoon, saddened by the idea that the delicious meal Penny had prepared could never be enjoyed by her.

The red soup sloshed up the sides of the bowl, and the idea came to Edie.

"If we put some blood in the soup, then you could have some, right?"

"We're not putting blood in the soup." Penny's response was quick and definitive.

"But we could, right?" Edie pressed. "How much would you need?"

"No."

It was clear that Penny was adamantly against the idea, and the rejection stung.

"Why not?" Edie asked. "Would it be too weird drinking my blood? Unappealing?"

"What?" Penny asked. "No. There is *nothing* unappealing about you. Believe me."

"Then what?" Edie asked. "I mean, you drink Empty's blood."

"That's simply transactional," Penny said. "With you, it would be different."

"Different how?"

Penny visibly thought through her words before responding. "It would be too intimate. It's not something either of us are ready for."

Edie wanted to press the matter more, but then when she

thought of Penny actually consuming some of her blood . . . well, it did feel like too much.

So, instead, she turned her focus back to her meal, mulling over the mess of emotions the discussion had brought up for her as she ate.

When she was finally so full she couldn't manage another bite, Edie got up and took her dishes to the sink.

"You're a really good person," Penny said.

Edie stood by the sink and regarded Penny. "Where did that come from?"

Penny shrugged. "I don't want you to feel rejected or think that I don't want you in any way. You're the only person that I've ever trusted enough to share the truth about myself with. You're special, and that's a relationship worth honoring and taking slowly."

"I'm just me," Edie said.

Penny held her gaze and Edie had to look away from the intensity she found there.

"There's no 'just' about it," Penny argued.

"I'm flying by the seat of my pants," Edie said. "I'm about to destroy my family's dream. I'm not out there saving lives or making big changes to the world. I make coffee."

"Maybe your coffee is exactly what the world needs," Penny argued.

"It's coffee," Edie stated.

"How different would the world be if people sat down with a pot of coffee and looked past their differences? I wish that there was a place where I could go, have a cup of coffee, and just belong. Don't you see what a rare and wonderful thing that is? You've created a space where people can exist, entirely as themselves. I haven't tried your coffee, and I'm sure it's wonderful, but let me tell you, it's the community you've created that makes your shop special."

"I'm glad you think my shop is important," Edie said. "I just need to find a way to save it."

"You're going to start with the Draculattes," Penny said. "You're going to bring in a little whimsy and go from there."

Edie smiled, glad she had Penny's full approval, before pushing away from the counter and going to where Penny still sat by the kitchen island. She closed the gap between them, kissing Penny slowly and sweetly.

When Penny's hands found her hips, pulling her closer, teasing up her sides, the kiss flared up in intensity. Edie kissed Penny with fervor, desperate for more, and Penny matched her desperation, drinking Edie in.

Penny had just begun kissing her way down Edie's neck and shoulder when Empty and Sid decided to burst into the apartment, giggling and kissing their way to the kitchen, not even seeming to notice that Edie and Penny were there.

"Empty!" Edie said. "I told you that I need the apartment for my date tonight, remember?"

"And we went out. Our movie's over," Empty protested. "Where else are we supposed to go? I live here, remember?"

Edie sent an apologetic gaze Penny's way.

"We'll stay out of your way," Empty promised. "Come on, Sid."

The two of them made their exit, heading to Empty's room, but a minute later the loud music shook the apartment, and Edie knew that any romance between her and Penny was over for the evening.

"Want to watch a movie or something?" Edie asked. "We can put on the subtitles, since we won't be able to hear a thing."

Penny laughed, but she nodded and followed Edie to the living room.

It wasn't going to be the sexy night that she'd envisioned, but still, the evening was cozy and nice, and she found herself happy for any time with Penny she could get.

The next day it would be back to work. And it would be time to launch the Draculatte infographics.

She curled up next to Penny, happy with the trajectory everything was taking.

Blood Lust, Immortality, and Curses, Oh My!

"Today's the day, eh?" Penny asked, leaning against the counter as Edie set up the placards that announced the Draculattes.

Edie had received zero buzz from the social media posts advertising her new Halloween beverage, but she was still excited for its launch day and how the drink would be received in person. Personally, she found it to be genius, but impressing herself with her own wit didn't guarantee sales.

"I wish the first official Draculatte could go to you," Edie said. "You were the inspiration, after all."

Penny leaned in and gave Edie a quick kiss that left her with a silly grin plastered across her face.

"I wish it too," Penny said. "But you're going to kill it today."

"I'm really grateful that I met you," Edie said. "I don't know if I've told you that yet. You make me happy, and it feels like maybe this one good thing could snowball into other good things. Like my luck is finally turning."

Penny gave her a sweet smile that communicated even more than the words that followed. "I'm really grateful that I met you, too. I feel seen for the first time in decades."

Edie melted a little at the tenderness she was met with.

Then, all too soon, Penny stepped back and said, "I should get going. The sun is going to be coming up soon."

Edie wanted to argue, but a look out the window at the gradually lightening sky told her that Penny had actually already visited with her for too long.

Edie gave a sad nod and a quick kiss to Penny, and watched as Penny headed off into the last stretch of night before turning the sign on her shop door to "OPEN."

The early mornings were always slow, and Edie took the time to enjoy the quiet and think about the wild ride she'd been on over the past few months. After feeling as though she'd been drowning since her parents death, she finally felt like she was able to take in some air, but while she felt like she'd been able to get her head above water, she also felt as though she was being carried with a current that was taking her in a wildly different direction than expected, and she didn't know whether or not she was going to be carried safely to calmer water or whether she was about to go over a massive waterfall.

Either way, she felt a little excitement as the first customer for the day stepped into her shop. He chuckled at the Draculatte sign, but didn't order the drink, opting instead for a regular black coffee to go.

It took a few customers before she got her first Draculatte order, and Edie thrilled at hearing the chuckle in the woman's voice as she ordered the drink. She took extra care to ensure it looked just right in hopes that the woman would take a photo of it to throw on Instagram and help further the word about the drink, but she simply chuckled at the drink and then took a dip before putting the lid on top and heading out the door.

The slow morning trickle of customers saw a few more ordering the Draculatte, but most continued to order their regular drinks. While her Halloween creation seemed to be attracting some interest, it wasn't garnering the buzz she'd hoped for.

Come on, Edie wanted to say, *it's called a Draculatte! It's funny!*

But maybe her pun wasn't as clever as she thought it was, and her mind was clouded with her desperation.

It's only day one, she reminded herself. It would take time to see if this marketing idea was going to gain any traction. She couldn't judge its success from the first hour of sales.

The pair of women came in just before the day shift came in to take over for Edie, and she frowned when she saw them enter the shop. They didn't come every week, but they were familiar enough. Whenever she overheard their conversations, they were gossiping about someone; they never cleared their dishes when they left; and in the summers they brought their school-aged kids who ran amok around the shop, stealing sugar packets, building houses out of coffee stir sticks, and bickering loudly with one another.

"Draculatte?" the one woman asked with a sneer as she approached the counter. "Haven't we had enough vampire hysteria in this city?"

"It's our new Halloween drink," Edie said as brightly as she could manage. "It's blond roast espresso with oat milk and raspberry, whipped cream, and raspberry 'blood drops.'"

"Pass," the woman said with a flat disinterest.

Her friend had an Ellora Merriweather novel peeking out of her purse— the next closest thing to a Bible in their city. If Ellora drank Draculattes, the place would be packed.

The woman turned to her friend. "Let's go to the *Jimmies* at the end of the block. I don't think I want to support any vampire resurgence."

"Vampire resurgence?" Edie asked, unable to contain the question. "I'm sorry. It's a punny Halloween drink. That's it."

The woman's eyes were full of spite as she met Edie's gaze, a level of spite that Edie was sure came from something bigger than her shop and its vampire-themed marketing ploy.

"I don't want my kids growing up thinking that vampires are funny or cool. Those *Nightfall* books promoted all kinds of toxicity. They were banned for a reason. One minute this city was a happy place to raise a family, and the release of those novels brought a flood of black clothing, piercings and tattoos, and children talking about blood lust, immortality, and curses. I don't know about you, but I don't want my kids growing up thinking that lifestyle is normal."

Edie wanted to say something about the Ellora Merriweather novel in the friend's purse. Those books were known for their "wholesome values," but who got to define what was wholesome and what wasn't? The hatred that the women were spewing over a Halloween drink hardly seemed like something Edie would have wanted her hypothetical children exposed to. She'd prefer the black clothing, piercings, and tattoos to hatred any day.

"Shall I take it you don't want to try the corruption cortado or the murder matcha, then?" Edie asked.

The woman gaped at her, struggling to find words for a long moment, before she sputtered, "We will be taking our business permanently elsewhere. And rest assured I will be advising everyone else I know to do the same."

Edie smiled and waved them goodbye, and as soon as they turned to leave, she rolled her eyes and flipped them the middle finger behind their backs. When the door closed behind them, she let out a long breath of frustration.

Indignation burned within her at their outsized reaction to a drink with some raspberry syrup drops on top of the whipped cream. Had she not known Penny, she might have laughed off the intensity of their over-exaggeration. But if they had that to say about a drink, what would they say if they knew the truth about Penny?

Edie had come out as a lesbian nearly ten years earlier, but before she'd claimed her truth, she had been a scared teenager, worried about what the world would say. Even before she had come out to her parents, they'd had a rainbow pride sticker on their shop window. One day, right around the time she was aching with both desperation and terror over the thought of being true to herself, her family had gone into work to find the sticker had been scratched off the shop window. The women's reaction to her Draculatte brought back the physical sensations of fear and shame she'd felt then. She knew how Penny would feel.

And the fear and shame morphed into a white-hot rage.

Her parents had responded by mounting a large pride flag above the walk-up window.

Edie wasn't sure what the equivalent response for her would be yet, but she'd be damned if she let them bully her into assimilation.

Because damn it, her coffee shop deserved to be a place for everyone. Penny included.

Friends Don't Let Friends Drink Instant Coffee

Edie went home from her morning shift all fired up, with no idea how she could funnel her anger into something productive, which was, perhaps, why, when she walked past her kitchen toward the bedroom, she was so bothered by the sight in front of her.

"No," she said, stopping Empty in her tracks. "I can't let you do that."

Empty had an almost-comical look of deer-in-headlights. "You can't let me what? Make coffee?"

"*That* is not coffee," Edie said, and she didn't hesitate to take the cup from Empty's hands and pour the instant caffeine sludge down the sink.

"Hey!" Empty protested. "What are you doing?"

"I'm making you a proper coffee." Edie went to the cupboard where she stored all her beans. "What do you like? Light roast? Dark?"

"I like my French Vanilla Quick Perk."

Edie let out a sigh. It was as if everything Empty said and

did was designed specifically to get on her nerves.

"You know what, I'll go with the medium roast."

She pulled the beans out of the cupboard, ground a couple of tablespoons with the electric grinder, and added them to the French press that she kept on the counter. The kettle was already full of boiling water from the atrocity that Empty had been making, and she added the water on top of the coffee grounds.

"Give it a minute," Edie said.

Empty rolled her eyes but went to the dining room table and took a seat to wait for her coffee.

"Listen," Edie said, "I'm the coffee expert. Trust me on this one. You'll never drink that swill again."

Silence stretched between them awkwardly as they waited for the coffee to brew. Anger at the two women and their ridiculous leap in logic still simmered within her, and her heart went out to Empty, who would have been exactly the type of person to shoulder the brunt of their petty judgment. Guilt at her own judgments cast upon Empty added to her discomfort. Empty was a little . . . alternative, but she was a sweet girl underneath her spooky exterior.

"So, what is it you do for work?" Edie realized she knew very little about Empty, having only asked for the month's rent in cash before giving her the keys.

Empty pulled at the frayed edges of her sleeves. "I'm not really working right now. I mean, I've looked, but there aren't a lot of places hiring. The few places I've interviewed for, I haven't heard back from."

"What do you want to do?" Edie asked.

"I don't know," Empty mumbled with a shrug. "Anything, really. I'd love to not have to rely on my asshole parents for rent money. They won't let me live with them, but they'll make sure

I'm not destitute. Kind, right? They just sign cheques to assuage their guilt. I'd rather they keep every ounce of guilt they may have."

Edie nodded along, opting not to comment.

"Anyway, I really wanted the bookstore job I applied for, but alas . . ." Empty trailed off, letting Edie fill in the rest. "Probably for the best. I really only want to sell the horror books. I'd rather travel back in time and attend my shitshow of a prom again than help sell Ellora Merriweather's flowery romance crap."

"Aren't at least half your vampire novels romance novels?" Edie asked, even though she knew it would have been wiser to keep quiet.

"Those are edgy."

Edie tried to look sincere as she nodded.

"Anyway, I guess I probably shouldn't have said all of that in my interview, but to be fair, they asked what books I'm into."

"Next time, just list a few titles of books you like."

Edie pushed the handle of the French press down, filtering the grounds from the fresh coffee, and then she poured herself and Empty each a cup.

"What do you take in your coffee?"

"French vanilla Quick Perk, remember?" Empty reminded her. "It comes with all the creamer and sugar that I need already mixed in. Plus, it tastes like French vanilla."

"Right," Edie said, and she added both cream and sugar in generous amounts to Empty's coffee. Nothing to her own. She didn't believe in masking the taste. She passed Empty's cup across the table to her and waited expectantly while Empty took a sip.

Empty grimaced. "It's so bitter."

"What?" Edie asked, and she took a sip of her own coffee as

a taste test. She knew the exact amount of grounds to add to her French press, so it didn't seem likely that she'd added too much, but she *was* having an off day.

The coffee tasted fine. No, better than fine. It was perfection.

"If you don't mind, I think I'll make myself a cup of instant," Empty said, pushing her mug away from her.

Edie did mind. She minded with every fiber of her being. But she said nothing, her jaw clenching as she nodded.

"Hey!" Empty said, as she got up to put more water in the kettle. "Are you hiring?"

A snort of a laugh burst from Edie before she could catch it.

"I'm sorry," she said immediately at Empty's hurt expression. "I didn't mean to laugh. It's just . . ." She paused to try to find a way to make this about her and not Empty. "The shop has been really struggling financially. I can hardly afford to employ myself." Not a lie.

Empty looked at her with empathy in her eyes, and then she opened her mouth and said, "Yeah, that tracks. Sorry, but your coffee tastes like motor oil."

"It's not . . . That's not . . ." Edie stammered as she tried to calm herself enough to form a reply. "The coffee sells fine. It's the shop itself. My great-grandparents built it. It needs a bit of modernization."

A complete overhaul was more like it, but Empty didn't need to know that.

Empty stirred her Quick Perk instant sugar powder into her hot water and came back to the table, visibly thinking over Edie's words.

"You should do something edgy," Empty offered, as though Edie had gone to her for suggestions. "Set yourself apart from all of the other coffee shops catering to soccer moms and hipsters."

"Oh yeah?" Edie asked, more out of amusement than curiosity. "Like how?"

"You could make it all goth or something. I know you were weirded out by Sid and me, but vampires actually have a huge following right now."

"A vampire coffee shop?" Edie asked. She thought about the ridiculous overreaction the two women had had to her Draculattes and she couldn't help but smile at the thought of how they'd react if she rebranded her entire shop.

Empty shrugged one shoulder. "I'd visit it, even if you don't have my French vanilla Quick Perk."

"I'll tell you what," Edie said, as the idea began to take root in her mind, "I'll consider it."

Empty lit up, showing more emotion than in the entire time Edie had known her. "If you do, please hire me. I'll even work 'for experience.'" She made air quotes with her fingers.

"Of course," Edie said, all while telling herself, *Don't even think about it. This is not just a bad idea; this is the worst idea ever.*

The idea, however, sunk its teeth in. She couldn't tell if it was simply her earlier indignation talking, but she wasn't sure it mattered.

It was an idea, and that was more than she'd had in months.

Her family's dying legacy could use a bite of immortality, and it would send a message to anyone petty enough to be angered by something as minor as a beverage name.

Vampires weren't going anywhere, and neither was her family's coffee shop.

Our Blood's in It

Edie sprayed and wiped down the counters at the end of the evening, and in the quiet of the empty shop she found herself drawn into a childhood memory of sitting atop those counters while her mom cleaned. Her mom used to sing along to bands like Nirvana, Blur, and the Smashing Pumpkins while cleaning during the lulls throughout the day, and she had quizzed Edie about music trivia while she'd worked.

Her mom had always been a fierce defender of the punks, the dreamers, and the queers. She'd fought to be a voice for the marginalized. She had been an ally in every sense of the word, long before Edie had ever come out, and even as a young, closeted queer she'd warmed herself with the knowledge that she'd always have a home when she was ready to tell the world who she was.

She remembered her dad bringing her various lattes to sample as she sat there on that counter. Some had been delicious and had made the menu, and some had been disasters, but he'd never been afraid to try something new. He went big, taking risks because he'd loved the coffee shop and hadn't been afraid to put everything on the line for it. Even when it didn't pay off, like the roaster, he'd always tried.

Edie was heavy beneath the weight of her ancestors, and she was terrified of crumbling beneath that weight, letting them down and having the coffee shop fail. But it wasn't going to fail because she was too afraid to take risks, or because she pandered to the privileged. She knew in her gut that both of her parents would entirely embrace her plan for the shop even if it was a complete gamble.

The knock on the door interrupted her thoughts, and Edie felt herself both buoyed and anxious at the sight of Penny standing outside.

She set down her cleaning rag and opened the door, relaxing a little at the tender smile she was met with.

"Come on in," Edie said.

Penny studied her but made no move to step inside. "There's something I have to do first," she said, and she closed the distance between the two of them, tracing cool fingers over Edie's cheek before capturing Edie's lips with her own.

Edie inhaled sharply, and then sank into the kiss, luxuriating in the softness of Penny's body pressed against her own, and the feel of Penny's tongue as it teased across her lip.

She felt a little dazed when Penny broke the kiss and stepped back.

"What was that for?" Edie asked.

One side of Penny's mouth quirked up into a smile. "I missed you a bit."

"Oh yeah?" Edie asked.

Penny held two fingers close together. "Like, a little."

Edie felt the flirtation settle warm in her chest, and maybe it was the infatuation talking, but that warm feeling reinforced what Edie was about to do.

"As much as I want to stand here and kiss you all night, there's something else I want to do," Edie said, and she took Penny's hand, leading her into the shop.

Edie's heart pounded as she led Penny behind the counter and pulled a mug down from the rack. She went to the sink and washed her hands, taking time to scrub them thoroughly beneath warm water, before drying them well with a soft, clean dishcloth.

"What are you doing?" Penny asked, her voice light and playful . . . until Edie pulled the knife out of the drawer. She asked again, a note of panic to her voice, "What are you doing?"

"I want to make you a coffee." Edie wanted to sound confident and sure, but she heard the slight quiver of fear in her voice.

Penny put her hands on Edie's, stilling her for a moment.

"Edie, look at me," Penny instructed.

Edie looked up. Penny's eyes were darker than usual, and she could see the storm of emotion.

"Why are you doing this?" Penny asked.

Edie's heart thundered in her chest. "Because I want to," she said. There was more to it than that, and she would get to the rest later. "Because you deserve to be able to go out for coffee."

She watched the conflicting feelings play out across Penny's face: concern, care, sadness, desire . . .

"Please?" Edie asked.

The desire won out, and Penny let go of Edie's hands. "You're doing this of your own accord," Penny said. "I didn't push you."

"Push me?" Edie asked with a laugh. "You didn't even so much as suggest this. This is all on me."

Penny nodded.

Edie brought the knife up and pressed it against her left

palm. Her right hand shook a little and she tried to exhale her nerves so the blade would still. Then, she readied herself, pressed down firmly, and drew the knife quickly across her palm.

Blood welled to the surface of her hand, and Edie quickly tipped her palm over the round, white coffee mug, the blood hitting the ceramic base in fat, messy droplets. She waited patiently as the blood dripped into the mug, dark and viscous. As it slowed, she squeezed the flesh of her palm to coax out a few more rich droplets.

"Is that enough?" Edie asked, frowning down at the mug.

She looked to Penny, whose eyes were closed as she took long, deep breaths, visibly exhaling each one.

"Penny," she said, and Penny's eyes opened. "Is that enough?"

Penny looked into the mug and managed a nod. When her eyes met Edie's, this time the storm was pure desire. She took Edie's hand in hers and said, "I want to taste you."

Edie had only ever imagined hearing those words in a much different context, but the impact was the same, and she swallowed hard and nodded.

Penny raised Edie's hand to her lips, and she carefully licked away the last of the blood before kissing Edie's palm.

The moment was tender and sensual, and Edie felt her own desire pool within her.

Penny released Edie's hand and stepped back. "I'm sorry," she said, and Edie picked up the undertone of embarrassment in Penny's voice. "I couldn't resist."

"I'm doing this for you," Edie said. She indicated the mug. "There's nothing to be embarrassed about."

Penny nodded unconvincingly.

Edie added two pumps of vanilla syrup and then used a wooden stir stick to mix it into the blood. Then, she dosed the coffee grounds into the portafilter before pulling the espresso shot. The familiar actions added some semblance of normalcy to the evening, and Edie grounded herself by watching the espresso drip from the twin spouts of the group head.

The scent of coffee filled the air, masking the heavy iron scent of blood, for which Edie was grateful.

Once the espresso finished, Edie poured milk into the metal mug, which she lifted to the steamer wand. The steam hit the milk with a satisfying hiss, and Edie was careful to steam it just right to create the perfect microfoam. She then poured the milk into the coffee, her stomach twisting violently at the blush of red that colored the latte.

Still, she kept her hand steady and created a perfect heart atop the drink. Then, she presented it proudly to Penny.

"Here you go," she said.

Penny gazed at Edie for a long moment, tenderness and appreciation visible in the softness of her gaze, and then she took the drink and brought it to her lips, taking a slow sip of the warm beverage. Her eyes fluttered closed of their own volition as the coffee hit her mouth.

"Oh my God." The words came out in a breathy sigh. She took another sip.

Edie flushed with pride. "You like it?" She'd been so bogged down in debt and shame since acquiring the shop, but in that moment, seeing Penny's reaction, she was reminded of her passion for the coffee itself.

It's in our blood. She felt a delirious joy and madness bubble up within her, and she laughed out loud.

"What's so funny?" Penny asked.

"Our slogan," Edie said, still bemused. "It's got it backwards. It's not in our blood; our blood's in it."

At this Penny laughed along with her and took another long drink of the latte. "Maybe it's both," she said. "It's been a few decades, but I've had lattes before, and none have been this good."

"I'm glad you think so," Edie said.

She was about to segue into her pitch for her plans for the coffee shop, but before she could say more, Penny was setting her mug down on the counter, stepping forward and pulling Edie into a kiss.

For the most part, she tasted of coffee and vanilla, *thank God*, but there was a slightly metallic undertone that Edie found herself very aware of.

But then, Penny's tongue teased her upper lip, and Edie found her mind going blank to everything except the incredible sensations that came with kissing Penny.

Her entire body melted into the kiss, and she was only distantly aware of the counter behind her as Penny pressed her against it.

"I know you have to be back here in just a few short hours," Penny said, breaking the kiss, though remaining pressed against Edie, "but would you like to come back to my place in the meantime?"

Edie nodded, unable to find any words as her heart hammered in her throat.

Penny smiled and stepped back, and Edie instantly missed the contact.

Penny finished the latte that Edie had made, and Edie washed the cup quickly before locking up and following Penny out into the night.

"I'm only a few blocks away," Penny said.

Sure enough, it was only a few minutes before Penny turned

off the sidewalk to the front step of a small bungalow with soft blue siding and a dark blue door.

Wherever Edie had envisioned Penny living, this was not it. Autumn leaves blanketed the garden, but there were a few chrysanthemums still flowering from planters, lit up beneath decorative solar lights: butterflies, dragonflies, and ladybugs.

"Wow," Edie said.

"You should see the garden in summer." The pride was clear in Penny's voice. "I have every variety of lilies, daffodils, and poppies. I'm down to my final late-season flowers."

"I can only imagine," Edie said. "It's stunning now."

"I take my solar lights and planters everywhere I go." The pride was evident in Penny's voice. "The first thing I do when I get to a new place is try to set up a halfway decent outdoor space."

"Um, this is more than halfway decent." Edie had killed every houseplant she'd tried to care for.

She followed Penny up the steps to the small front porch, with string lights wrapped around the railing, and the cushioned porch swing practically called Edie's name, begging for her to sit and watch the sunrise from that delightful-looking seat.

She sank down into the swing and rocked back and forth a couple of times while she surveyed the beautiful yard before her. For a brief instant, she pictured Penny sitting there with a morning coffee, and the thought was followed immediately by a sadness at the realization that the porch swing sat abandoned during the daytime.

Penny unlocked her front door, opened it, and leaned against it. Edie looked up to find Penny studying her with a tender smile.

"Come in?" Penny asked, almost shyly, which had never

been a word Edie had attributed to Penny.

Edie stood with a nervous excitement and followed Penny into the house.

Penny took Edie's jacket, and while she hung the coat in the entry closet, Edie took in her surroundings. To her left was the living room, and it was well-lit with various lamps: two floor lamps in the corners by the windows; a small vintage table lamp between the sofa and the love seat; and a small, angled reading lamp next to the recliner. Each of the lamps gave off a complementary soft, warm glow, which layered upon one another.

The windows had blue curtains that were tightly drawn, but even so Edie could see the blackout shades that had been pulled down behind the decorative coverings, offering a dual level of protection against the sunlight.

While it had been clear from the outside of the home that Penny had a green thumb and loved plants, the houseplants that filled Penny's home were all artificial. They were high-quality fake plants, but it was still clear they were plastic alternatives to the real thing. Real plants had the odd yellowing or droopy leaves; these ones were all too perfect, void of *life*. Edie ran her fingers over the plastic leaves of the fake fern next to her.

"It's hard to have real plants when you can't let any sunlight into the house," Penny said. "During the summer, I spend a lot of time in my garden outside. The plants can grow and thrive during the day, and I can enjoy their beauty while sitting outside at night."

"And in the winter?" Edie asked. The weather was already dipping to the freezing mark at night, and their northern climate practically promised that they would have snow within the month.

"Winters have different perks," Penny said. "Short days and long nights mean more time when I can exist in the world. I ski in the evenings after sunset with plenty of time before the hills close. I play hockey on a rec league. I chase the northern lights. In the winter, I have the chance to feel human again. I have the chance to *belong*."

Edie's heart ached for Penny. "But what about summers?" she asked.

Penny gave a sad shrug. "I'd rather live somewhere where I can really be a part of society for six months of the year than somewhere where I feel like I'm on the outs year-round. The short nights make summers difficult. I work casual shifts and take summers off because there aren't enough nighttime hours to work a full shift. The *really* short days only last a couple months, though. It's a trade-off I've chosen to make."

Edie took off her shoes and followed Penny into her living room, continuing to take in all the decor. A colorful granny-square blanket draped over the back of the sofa, and other bright crocheted blankets clung to the backs of the other chairs in the room.

"Did you make these?" Edie asked, taking the corner of one blanket between her fingers and thumb. It was soft and well-worn.

"That one was made by my grandma, but the others, yes."

Penny had always seemed cool and edgy, a little dangerous perhaps. Her home was all color and warmth. She crocheted and gardened.

The far wall was decorated with framed photos, which hung above a wood fireplace with a cream-colored shag carpet resting in front of it.

Edie went to look at all the photos, finding various images

of Penny, smiling in the sunshine, a look of joy on her face unlike anything Edie had ever seen on her before. She wore the joy like a glove. Edie longed to see that look on Penny's face in person.

"Those were all before . . ." Penny said.

Edie picked up a free-standing photo off the mantel and ran her fingers over the frame, gazing at Penny in a one-piece bathing suit, standing in the surf of the ocean, a bright grin on her face, the sun highlighting gold streaks that Edie had never noticed before in Penny's otherwise dark hair.

"California," Penny said, stepping up beside Edie, taking the photo, and setting it back on the mantel.

She knelt down, picking up a couple of logs which she arranged inside of the fireplace. She set some small splinters of kindling and newspaper in with the logs, and Edie watched as she effortlessly lit the fire with a match, filling the room with a gentle warmth and the comforting scent of burning wood.

Then, she turned off some of the lamps in the room, the firelight filling the space, making it intimate.

Penny moved to the sofa and motioned for Edie to join her, but as eager as she was to settle into the intimacy, the photos had sparked too much of curiosity in her. She wanted to look at them all, to know more, to know Penny.

"You're human in all of these photos," Edie commented. "I mean, I always knew that you were a human before you became a vampire, but to see you *before* . . ." She trailed off, not sure how to put words to the deep pull she felt in her chest. "How did you end up becoming a vampire?"

"It's a long story," was all Penny supplied.

Edie looked down at where Penny sat, noting the way the light from the flame flickered with soft gold tones across Penny's skin. "We have all the time in the world."

Penny worked the corner of her granny-square afghan between her fingers, her gaze fixed on the blanket, as her brow furrowed in pain at the memory.

"I got sick," Penny said. "That was the start of it. I was out there living life to its fullest. I was living out of a van, traveling North America, visiting beaches and national parks, hiking, surfing, kayaking. If it was outdoors, in the sunshine, I was out there trying it."

Edie had no trouble envisioning Penny diving into every activity. She'd have been good at them all, Edie knew.

"And then I got diagnosed with melanoma. Turns out, even as a human, the sun wanted to kill me."

Penny said the words with a bitter chuckle that betrayed her level of pain.

"Anyway, while I was in the hospital, I had a night shift nurse, Marguerite. The two of us connected right away. She was funny, with a dry wit a bit like you, and her morbid sense of humor made all the treatments halfway tolerable. I was dying. It was shit timing to fall in love. But I fell for her hard and fast anyway."

Penny paused and Edie could see the pain etched in her features.

"I didn't know the truth about her. At least, not before . . ." Even now, decades later, it was clear that Penny was still processing all that had happened. "Had I known, I would have never . . ."

"She was a vampire," Edie said, filling in the gaps in the story for Penny.

Penny nodded. "She was. And my very human sickness was making me weaker by the day."

Edie couldn't imagine Penny lying in a hospital bed. The

thought made her stomach curdle.

"I wasn't going to get better. We both knew that. I'd accepted it." Penny was quiet for a long moment, and her voice was small when she continued. "She didn't. She wasn't ready to say goodbye, and she had the power to keep me alive with her." She paused and repeated the word with air quotes: "Alive."

"She saved you," Edie said.

"She cursed me," Penny argued, tears welling in her eyes. "Look around. This house is a prison. I can't let even a sliver of sunlight in. I never wanted this. I would have rather died."

The pain was palpable, and Edie kept silent, partly because there were no words that would make any of it better for Penny, and partly because she was profoundly glad that Penny hadn't died.

"Nothing's felt like living since that night," Penny said, and then she raised her eyes to Edie. "Until meeting you."

Edie's cheeks warmed, and she knew it wasn't from the fire she still stood next to. "I'm just me. Pretty ordinary." She enunciated each of the last two words and turned back to the rest of the photos on the mantel.

Then Penny was next to her, resting her hand on the small of her back, and the warmth settled much lower in her body.

"Edie McLean," Penny said, and Edie turned to meet her burning gaze. "You are anything but ordinary."

Edie opened her mouth to protest, but Penny was quick to cut her off.

"I knew you were special the minute I met you."

"Some kind of vampire sense?" Edie joked.

"No," Penny stated, her voice still serious as she tried to make her point despite Edie's defenses. "Regular old observation. Anyone can see how special you are."

127

"That's not true," Edie argued.

"It is, though."

Edie didn't know how to simply accept the compliment, and Penny took her silence as an opening to continue stressing her point.

"I work casual shifts with different people each night. I've made it a habit to bring coffee with me to my shifts. Like you, I've learned that coffee brings people together. The first night I met you—and it couldn't have been too long after your parents passed—you greeted me with the brightest smile I've ever seen, and I was captivated."

"Yeah, but that's because I thought you were hot," Edie teased.

Penny wasn't letting her off the hook. "No, it wasn't. Once you really noticed me, you got all shy. It was before that, that I really saw how you glow. I've watched you with your customers. You're like that with everyone. It doesn't even matter that you've been drowning in grief, or that your family's shop is on the brink of bankruptcy, and you're stressed to the max. Each person you greet, you take a moment to smile at them like they're the only person that matters in that moment."

Edie's blush burned.

"I've seen you give your leftover pastries at the end of the night to the man who sits out there on the corner."

"Hank," Edie corrected, habitually.

"See?" Penny stressed. "You know his name. Do you know what other people are doing? They're pulling their kids close when they walk past him, moving to the far side of the sidewalk and avoiding eye contact. Businesses are calling the police to have him displaced. Sent anywhere other than in front of their shop."

"Basic kindness," Edie tried to argue, but Penny kept going.

"I've seen the way Empty and Sid get under your skin, and yet you've never cast judgment."

"I've cast some judgment," Edie argued.

"Well, you've continued to treat them with kindness, and let me tell you, I've seen the harsh way the world greets those who are different."

Edie didn't know what to say. Penny was standing there listing the reasons she thought she was special, but basic human kindness should have been the most ordinary thing about her.

"There was a reason I felt safe enough to tell you the truth about me," Penny said. "You've made me feel welcomed as my whole self. Before you, I was adrift. I didn't know where I could belong. You've given me a place to land."

Edie held Penny's gaze for only a moment more before her eyes fluttered shut and Penny's lips brushed softly over hers.

The kiss started out soft, tentative, and yearning, and then Penny poured the same bruising intensity that her words had held into the kiss. Edie's breath caught in her chest. She leaned into the kiss, gasping a little as Penny's tongue grazed across her lips.

Penny pulled back and her eyes held a fire that made Edie melt. She saw the question and the desire in Penny's gaze and nodded her response.

Beside them, the fire crackled, warming their skin as they removed one another's clothes. Edie only had a moment to admire Penny, though, because Penny's lips were on hers again, and Edie sank into the kiss, giving herself over to the moment entirely.

Bathed in the soft firelight, Edie lay curled around Penny, one of the colorful crocheted afghans draped loosely over their lower halves. She traced her fingers up Penny's side and down her bare chest, following the flicker of shadows that danced over her gentle curves and contours.

Penny thought her vampirism was a curse. Edie tried to empathize, but vampirism had brought the two of them together across what would have otherwise been an unbridgeable chasm of time. It was a marvel that they were lying there together, and she couldn't bring herself to see it as anything less.

"What are you thinking?" Penny asked.

Edie's head rested on Penny's shoulder, and she tilted her chin to gaze up at Penny who stroked her hair in response.

"Dirty thoughts," Edie admitted.

Penny laughed and pulled Edie tighter to her.

"If only you didn't have to work today," Penny said. "We could keep those blackout curtains drawn and lie here by the fire all day."

"Speaking of work—"Edie began, but Penny's laughter interrupted her.

"Really? You want to segue to talk of work now?" Flirty amusement underscored Penny's words.

Edie chuckled, but she was undeterred despite her desire to spend the day getting lost in Penny's touch. "It's important. I promise."

Penny kissed the top of her head, causing a little flutter in her chest. "I'm listening."

Edie sat up and struggled in her search for the right words

as Penny rested her hands behind her head, her naked chest calling to Edie.

"I had a bit of a wild idea," Edie began. "You're going to want to shoot it down, but please hear me out before you do."

At this, the flirty smile fell from Penny's face, and she sat up as well, brows furrowing with concern.

"Don't you think it was a strange coincidence, the way you, Empty, and I all came into one another's lives?" Edie asked.

"It *was* a bit serendipitous."

"It was more than serendipity." Edie held Penny's gaze despite the wariness she saw there. "We came together for a reason. If not for Empty, I wouldn't know the truth about you, and we wouldn't be here, would we?"

"I don't know," Penny hedged.

But Edie did. Penny had spent decades hiding herself, and for good reason, but there couldn't have been true intimacy between the two of them without Edie knowing such a huge part of Penny's identity.

"Empty's fictional world gave you a safe place to live out your reality," Edie continued. "And both of you have opened my eyes to communities I'd known nothing about."

"Where are you going with this?" Penny asked.

"I want to do more than market Draculattes for Halloween. This is bigger than a punny drink. I want to rebrand all the drinks, redecorate, make my family's shop entirely vampire-themed, and I want to serve blood-based lattes to the real vampires in this city. I want you, and others like you, to have a place where you can gather and grab a coffee."

"Hold up," Penny said. "Do you hear how ridiculous that sounds? You want to brand your coffee shop—your family's pride and joy for generations—around fictional vampires as a front for serving blood-laced beverages to real vampires?"

"Yes." It did sound ridiculous, but Edie felt steady in her decision.

"You know our city hates vampires, right? You're aware of how swiftly the *Nightfall* book series was banned? Can you imagine what would happen if it was discovered you were serving drinks with human blood mixed in? Why risk it?"

"Simply put, you're worth the risk," Edie answered. "I reject the idea that there isn't a place for you in this world. I want to change that. I want to make a place for you."

Emotion welled in Penny's eyes, and it was thick in her voice when she spoke. "Then why not secretly serve blood beverages without the fictional vampire front?"

"First of all, for the same reason you get your blood from Empty in the first place. There's a degree of safety in hiding in plain sight. But also, because to hell with this city and the narrow-mindedness and silly judgment. I want a degree of visibility to push back against those beliefs without exposing your community and putting you all at risk."

She could feel the fear radiating from Penny, and she fought against internalizing it. This was the right course of action. She felt certain about that.

"Fictional vampires aren't going to make people more accepting toward real vampires." Penny's voice was small and sad.

Edie rejected that defeat. "Why not? Fiction has always illuminated truths about the world. Look at queer stories: we were villainized, then our stories were tragedies, and now we exist in art in complex ways, rich with possibilities for our lives."

She saw a note of wistfulness underlying the fear in Penny's eyes and latched onto that.

"I want to give our city the story of a vampire coffee shop. A little piece of pretend until the thought of the real deal isn't such a scary leap. And in the meantime, there can be at least one place where you don't have to hide your truth. You can drink lattes and simply exist."

Penny looked away as tears filled her eyes.

"Let me do this," Edie pleaded.

"I don't want to be the reason your family's shop goes under," Penny argued, though there was less fight behind her words than when Edie had first pitched the idea.

"My family's shop is already going under, and I'd rather go under fighting for something I believe in."

Conflicting emotions visibly warred within Penny. Edie knew that what she was suggesting was no small ask, but she also knew it could be so worth the risk.

"Where are you going to get the blood for the drinks?" Penny asked at last.

Edie exhaled with relief and straightened to discuss the details.

"I was hoping you'd be able to help me with that. You said you don't need much blood to make food and drinks palatable, and that you have access to medical discard?"

"I can talk to my contact," Penny warily agreed.

Edie beamed. "This is going to be a good thing."

Penny chewed on her lower lip, but Edie could see that she was thinking over how to help make things work, instead of how to talk her out of the idea.

"You can charge a premium for the blood-based drinks," Penny said. "A steep premium. There should be compensation, given the risk involved, and besides, one of the perks of immortality is that we've had decades, or even centuries for some, to accumulate income."

"You think other vampires will come in and buy drinks?" Edie asked, the excitement now bubbling out of her.

"I can't make any promises," Penny said. "I can put the word out, but I have no idea what the reaction will be or if others will be willing to take the risk."

Edie tried not to let Penny's words discourage her.

"That latte was pretty damn delicious," Penny said. "And I'm certain I'm not the only one who has been lonely in this never-ending night."

Edie leaned forward and captured Penny's lips. A kiss full of equal parts empathy and optimism. When she pulled back, she said, "We can do this. We can."

Penny still looked hesitant, but Edie could be excited enough for them both.

Finally, Penny echoed quietly, "We can do this."

In Our Blood

Edie's excitement for renovating the McLean Family Coffee Shop lasted until the first family photo came down. She'd gone in amped and ready to make changes. Then she'd picked up the frame nearest the door, which held a photograph of her in her toddler years sitting atop her dad's shoulders with a wide grin on her face while her dad handed a latte to a customer, and the minute she'd lifted the frame from the wall, she'd burst into tears.

The family photos needed to go. Her parents and grandparents had decorated the shop as if it were the family living room. They'd probably been hoping to make the shop feel homey and inviting, but Edie's junior prom photo really didn't need to be displayed for the world. Based on the reviews, the too-personal decor landed anywhere from confusing to outright off-putting.

"I'm not getting rid of you," Edie promised her dad, as she traced her fingers over the picture. "You're the heart of this shop."

She carried the framed photo to the back and wiped away the tears that threatened from the corners of her eyes. Her entire family could be displayed proudly in the roasting room, where the coffee they took such pride in was crafted. Edie would still be surrounded with memories and the love of her family, and she could redecorate the main shop in a cohesive and purposeful manner.

The door chimed, and she walked back out front as Empty stepped inside, balancing an armful of framed art between her arms and her chin.

Edie rushed over to help her with the art, easing the pictures down onto one of the tables.

"Let me know what you think," Empty said.

Edie's palms were sweaty as she readied herself to look through the collection. She'd sent Empty shopping for vampire-themed artwork with the meager amount of cash she'd been able to scrape together, along with a little extra cash that Penny had chipped in. She'd known that her roommate would be the person best suited for finding such art, but though she'd warned Empty to keep it "coffee shop appropriate," she still expected her to return with either an armful of gory splatterpunk paintings depicting vampires feeding from lifeless human victims, or erotic blood fantasy photos showing vampires in various stages of undress sucking from the necks of their very willing "prey."

Her relief was tangible when she picked up the first piece of art to find a stylish black and white portrait of Bela Lugosi as Dracula. She set the portrait aside to look at the next one, then the next, pleasantly surprised as she was able to green-light every piece of art that Empty had selected. They were all classy black and white Gothic portraits: Dracula's castle surrounded by fog, bats flying in the night, a wooden coffin that was open just a crack . . . They leaned into the vampire motif, but they would give the shop a tasteful, artistic feel.

"These are perfect," Edie said.

Empty looked as if she was about to burst with pride. "You really think so?"

Edie didn't hesitate to nod her approval. "Absolutely."

When Edie had told Empty about the plan for the coffee shop, Empty's excitement had been palpable. She'd seen how important it was for the girl to have a place where she could belong. That excitement had helped buoy Edie's own optimism about the change. There were others like Empty in the city, she was sure. Others like Penny as well. Outsiders of one kind or another who would rally around a coffee shop that made space for them while society cast them out.

"What can I help with next?" Empty asked.

When Empty had immediately begged for a job in any capacity, be it work or volunteer, Edie had been reluctant to agree, but her roommate's eagerness was translating into a surprising level of work ethic that warranted more than the meager pay that Edie was able to offer. As soon as she could afford it, she knew she'd be increasing Empty's wage and work hours.

"If you're up for it, we can start repainting these walls," Edie said.

Empty nodded enthusiastically, and Edie wondered when the last time was that Empty had ever felt truly included in something.

They set to work pushing all the tables and chairs to the middle of the room, removing nails, taping edges, and laying down drop sheets. It was early afternoon by the time they dipped the first brush into the paint, and it was well into the night by the time they finally finished the painting.

Edie pulled the roller down the wall one final time and then stepped back, admiring the end result. Even with only artificial light, the sun having long set, Edie could tell that the place looked much improved. They had painted the walls a light gray, and the baseboards had all been repainted black. She had to wait for everything to dry before she could hang the art that Empty had brought, but she could easily envision the portraits on the walls and could tell that the place was going to give off a really clean, classy vibe. She could see the shop having appeal to customers regardless of whether they were interested in the goth vampire aesthetic. Unlike its previous decor, it now had a cohesive appearance and didn't appear confused and outdated.

"This place is totally badass," Empty said.

Edie nodded, taking it all in. "Heck yeah."

The door chimed and Edie turned at the sound, smiling as she watched Penny cross the threshold, eyes widening as she took in the transformed shop.

"Wow," Penny said, scanning her eyes around the room. "You've done a lot today."

"You haven't seen the half of it yet," Edie said. "Come in. Check out all this art that Empty picked up."

Empty stood a little taller beside her.

Penny moved to the table with the portraits and began looking at them slowly, one at a time.

"This place is going to be incredible," she said when she finished.

Pride bloomed in Edie's chest for the first time since her parents' death. She'd inherited this shop and all its shortcomings, and she was going to really make something of it.

"I'm going to keep all of the tables and chairs, but I'm going to reupholster the chairs and get rid of the floral print," Edie said. At Penny's look of skepticism, she added, "I've watched some YouTube videos. I think I can do it."

"I'll help you," Penny promised.

Edie had been counting on that, but she didn't admit as much, instead continuing to explain her plans.

"I spoke with the crochet club; they're excited by the idea for the shop and have agreed to crochet some lacy tablecloths. I'm thinking of hitting the thrift store to look for some lounge chairs and bookshelves to create a little reading nook over in that corner, the shelves filled with vampire fiction. Including the *Nightfall* series."

"I love it," Penny said, and the earnestness in her voice tugged at Edie, who swayed a little closer into the warmth and comfort of Penny's approval.

She wasn't numb to the emotional impact of all the changes she'd made. The shop had been her childhood home and it looked completely different now. However, she believed in the reason for the changes, so she buried the grief that threatened with each alteration.

"I made something for you," Penny said, almost hesitantly. "You don't have to use it. I won't be offended if you don't, but I think it would fit this place perfectly."

Edie's interest was piqued. "What is it?"

Penny answered by leaving Edie standing there confused while she went outside to collect whatever it was she'd brought.

She returned a moment later with what appeared to be a large wooden shop sign.

"What's this?" Edie asked. They'd repainted the letters on her shop sign less than two months earlier.

Penny set the sign face up on the table. A single word, "Bloodline," was painted in dark red lettering.

"Whoa," she heard Empty exclaim beside her, but Edie simply stared at the word, struggling to comprehend its purpose.

"We're the McLean Family Coffee Shop."

"Hear me out," Penny began.

But Edie shook her head. All the grief she'd been burying as she'd pressed forward with the changes began clawing out of her.

"At what point am I simply starting a whole new coffee shop? If I change the name, there's nothing left of my family's dream."

"That's not true," Penny argued.

Edie didn't want to listen. Panic and grief wrapped tight fingers around her throat. She looked around, desperately trying to ground herself with some familiarity, but the shop was all different. It wasn't home anymore.

"I need some air," she choked out, and she pushed outside, grateful for the autumn chill.

Hardly a moment later, she felt a hand on her back, and she closed her eyes at the soothing touch, allowing her breathing to gradually come back under control.

"The place will always be the McLean Family Coffee Shop," Penny said.

Edie didn't have it in her to argue, so she said nothing in response.

"All it has is a fresh coat of paint and some new wall art. Those surface things weren't what made your family's shop what it is. The place has thrived for generations in spite of the decor, not because of it."

Edie scoffed. "The place has thrived because of its convenient location and late hours. Let's not kid ourselves."

She wanted to believe that some of the McLean Family essence would permeate the shop no matter what, but the truth was, the place was just a building, and she'd changed everything about that building. Now, Penny was even suggesting they take the family name off it.

"After you suggested this big renovation, I took it upon myself to Google your family's coffee shop and read the Yelp reviews."

Edie cringed. She knew that the place had a low star rating and that most people seemed to find the shop ugly and strange.

"You know what?" Penny continued. "Any review that actually mentioned the coffee, said that it was possibly the best in the city. One particular review stood out to me. It said, 'The McLean family doesn't know the first thing about running a business, but damn do they roast good coffee.'"

Edie felt the first stirrings of pride. "My great-grandfather taught my grandfather everything he knew about roasting beans. My grandfather kept studying and experimenting and learning and then he taught my father everything he knew about roasting beans. My father further perfected the craft over the years, and I learned everything that I know from him."

"See?" Penny said. "It's like the old slogan said, 'Coffee's in your blood.'"

Edie felt the panic begin to subside. Change was scary, but it was also sometimes necessary.

She took a deep breath and made a decision.

"Help me hang the new sign," Edie said.

The McLean Family Coffee Shop was officially Bloodline.

Morphogenesis

After two weeks of renovations, Edie was beyond excited to relaunch the McLean Family Coffee Shop, now officially known by its moniker, Bloodline. The plan was to relaunch Bloodline on All Hallow's Eve, with a big launch party, complete with costumes and candy—a fun and whimsical evening to reintroduce her family's coffee shop to the city.

"When I said that you were going through a stage of morphogenesis, this was not quite what I meant." Blake stood in the doorway surveying all the changes for the first time with measured appraisal.

"But do you like it?" Edie asked, unsure how to gauge his reaction, as he went through the world with a constant air of elitism about him.

"I find the concept to be quite innovative," Blake answered, which was about the closest thing to a compliment that Edie had ever received from him. "But I'm a little disappointed you took it in such an uninspired direction. Where are the moral quandaries?"

"Moral quandaries?" Edie echoed.

"The moral agony involved in surviving off the lifeblood of

others, the curse of being eternally cast in darkness, and the utter torment of living forever while watching those around you all eventually succumb to the hands of time."

"You paint a grim picture," Edie said. "One that I'm not sure how to capture in a coffee shop."

"Have you heard of Edvard Munch?" Blake asked. "His painting, *Vampire*, would have made for much more intriguing wall art than an insipid portrait of Dracula's castle. It was originally titled '*Love and Pain*' and would be a perfect talking point for the torment involved."

"I'm not going for pain and torment here," Edie reminded him. "I'm going for a quirky but welcoming and all-inclusive coffee shop."

Blake studied the room again. "The place will have a certain commercial charm," he conceded.

"That's what I want to hear."

Edie loved Blake for his honesty, but she also knew not to take his opinion with much more than a grain of salt. She knew that he would have favored a highbrow coffee shop where only the intellectual elite gathered so that they could discuss deep ideas after dark. She hoped, however, that Blake could get behind the changes even if they were in a different direction than he'd have chosen for the place. He'd been a loyal staff member and a decent friend.

"So," Edie hedged, "are you still in?"

Blake rubbed the stubble on his cheek as he contemplated the question. "I'm not taking any of the night shifts," he answered. "I like the concept well enough, but I would like to continue my routine of meditation in the evenings."

"That's totally fair," Edie answered. She had changed the coffee shop hours to be open twenty-four hours a day Tuesdays through Saturdays in order to accommodate the vampire clientele she hoped to serve, but she wasn't looking for any help with the night shifts, wanting to keep the whole bloody beverage thing very much under wraps. Penny had put in her notice at the hospital so that she could assist Edie with the overnight shifts, a huge sacrifice in wages for something Penny was clearly coming to believe in.

Empty chose that moment to saunter in. Wordlessly, she shrugged out of her backpack and tossed it onto one of the lounge chairs before thumbing through the collection of novels that had been selected for the small bookshelf in the corner.

Edie suspected that her biggest challenge with Empty, aside from trying to get the girl to have some sort of appreciation for proper coffee, would be to get Empty to rein in her excitement and remember that she was staff, not a customer.

"Come over here and meet Blake," Edie said.

Empty was reading the back cover of one of the books, but she begrudgingly put the novel down and sauntered over to where Edie and Blake stood.

Blake, she noticed, looked down his nose at Empty with a look of much more careful appraisal than he'd given the shop.

They're going to be a fun pair, Edie thought, realizing that she'd probably be spending the first few weeks working round the clock just to ensure those two were able to work together with even the slightest bit of cohesion.

"Empty, Blake has been working here for years. When I'm not here, he's your go-to guy when it comes to making drinks and all things coffee."

"Got it," Empty said, but her tone as she studied Blake's condescending gaze said otherwise.

"Blake," Edie continued, "Empty's new to working in a coffee

144

shop, but she knows everything there is to know about vampires. She's going to be a major asset to our shop. She's already been a key player, helping behind the scenes with all the renovations."

It was almost comical the way Empty puffed with pride.

"Help each other out," Edie begged. "Trust in one another's expertise."

Blake held out his hand, and said a stiff, "Welcome aboard."

Empty looked to Edie before giving Blake's hand a lazy shake before shoving her hand back in her pocket.

"We have a new menu," Edie said, and she led the two to the folder she had on the counter that contained copies with detailed instructions on how to make each of the drinks. She handed each of them a copy.

She'd spoken with the writer's group the night before she'd closed the shop for the renovations, and they'd agreed to help her brainstorm menu items for the relaunch. For the most part, they'd all been intrigued by the idea immediately, but once they started coming up with drink names and puns, the brainstorming session had snowballed into a blizzard, with all of them leaping into the vampire coffee shop concept with gusto.

The London fog had been rebranded as the Transylvanian fog, the flat white had become the flatline white, the caramel macchiato had become the coronary macchiato, the salted caramel mocha had become the salted carotid mocha, and the cold brew was now known as the cold blood cold brew. For simple coffee, patrons could order an IV drip coffee, available in light- or dark-hearted.

She noticed Blake smirk as he read over the drink names, and she counted that as a major win.

"Empty, Blake and I will show you how to make the drinks, and we can spend the day practicing."

"Sure thing," Empty said.

"And Blake, while we teach Empty how to make all these beverages, she can fill you in on all of the latest vampire lore and fiction so that you're able to discuss appropriately if it comes up with customers. We want to be able to fully embrace this theme."

"I am familiar with vampire lore," Blake argued.

"Are you team Godric or team Aloysius?" Empty asked.

"Who?" Blake asked.

"Exactly," Edie said. "Empty's going to fill you in on all the must-knows about the most popular, influential, or highly regarded vampire novels. You're going to take it all in. Really learn your vampire subculture."

Blake didn't look enthused, but he didn't argue.

Edie walked over to the espresso machine and motioned for Empty to follow.

"Let's start by learning how to make a basic latte."

Her scrappy little team was pulling together.

The McLean Family Coffee Shop might not be immortal, but it damn well wasn't on its deathbed yet.

Late-Night Lewdness

Edie puttered around the coffee shop, eagerly watching the sky darken outside the window, her anticipation growing with each passing minute. In keeping with the new theme of the coffee shop, she'd listed the official relaunch time as "sundown," which made for a long day watching both the clock and the sky, unsure what to do with herself while she waited.

"If Aloysius was truly seeking redemption, though, how could he ever willingly impart the same cursed fate onto Seraphina?" Blake asked. He and Empty had both agreed to work the first few hours of the relaunch so that the entire team could be together for the reopening celebration, and they'd spent the prep time discussing the *Nightfall* book series with ridiculously impassioned opinions.

Empty took a moment to answer, pulling her lip ring between her teeth as she focused on the leaf she was trying to make in the top of the latte. She finished pouring the steamed milk, ending with an unsightly blob of frothed milk on top.

"Damn it," she muttered under her breath. Then, she turned her attention to Blake's question. "He loves her and can't imagine a life without her. Love makes people a little selfish sometimes."

"Love or infatuation? The way you tell it, the two hardly even know one another." Blake had agreed to read the *Nightfall* series for research purposes, and his curmudgeonly questions about the book had quickly morphed into real interest, leading to the development of a surprising new friendship between him and Empty.

"They have a soul connection," Empty stressed. She turned to Edie. "What am I doing wrong?"

Edie'd explained the milk frothing technique to Empty multiple times, but despite Empty's best efforts, she was not picking up the skill. "You need to lower the tip of the steamer wand a little more, so that you don't get such large air bubbles. You want it to kiss the surface of the milk in a way that sounds like ripping paper."

"Godric was, by far, the superior selection for Seraphina." Blake pressed on with the debate. "That he wasn't willing to compromise her soul, speaks volumes to his character."

The Godric versus Aloysius debate was made all the more ridiculous by the formal wear that they were all clothed in for the launch party. Blake had needed to borrow a suit from Edie's dad's old wardrobe, but despite his grumbling about the launch party dress code, he had run a comb through his usually unruly hair, and he was clean-shaven for the first time in all the years Edie had known him.

Empty wore a simple black dress, with black lipstick and heavy eyeliner, but despite the emo exterior, she radiated joy. Edie'd never seen her happier.

"It's a double-bind," Empty continued. "If Seraphina had ended up with Godric, he'd be guilty of the same selfishness that you're accusing Aloysius of."

"Well, I do think that Seraphina is ultimately better off

without either of them. However, Aloysius pursued Seraphina. At least if she ended up with Godric, it could have been of her own choice and free-will. And Godric wouldn't have sacrificed her soul by turning her into a vampire like Aloysius did."

"And how do you know that?" Empty pressed. "Godric wouldn't have been willing to watch Seraphina age and ultimately die any more than Aloysius would. Besides, who is really to say that her soul is damned because she's a vampire now."

Edie wanted to stab her eardrums to avoid having to listen to more of the *Nightfall* debate, and the rebranded shop was zero hours old.

Finally, the sun slipped below the horizon, and the sky faded from blue to black.

"You both ready?" Edie didn't wait for their answer to unlock the front door and flip the sign to open.

Edie had been unsure what to envision, and she'd known that the dream of having a lineup down the street was nothing more than a dream, but it was still anticlimactic to turn the deadbolt with a heavy clunk only to go back to puttering around an empty shop.

Her heart quickened when she finally heard door chimes, but then fell when she turned to see Sid saunter confidently inside.

"Would you take a look at this? You've done it! You've angered the Karens."

"What?" Edie asked.

Sid held out his cell phone for Edie to read the news article, and anger quickly flared within her as she read the bold type above the photo of her coffee shop with its new sign.

"LATE-NIGHT LATTE? MORE LIKE
LATE-NIGHT LEWDNESS!"'

149

Edie seethed. "Really? That's the best headline they could come up with?"

"I love it." Sid's delight was evident in the wide grin across his face. "Your quaint little family coffee shop is making waves in this uppity city."

Edie ignored him and read on, each word only enraging her further.

"Our innocent youth will go in seeking coffee and instead be served a warm cup of corruption. It's bad enough that vampires have gained such footing in the popular media, but to create an entire shop dedicated to these satanic creatures, with drinks glorifying the consumption of human blood is an entirely new depth of depravity and stands in stark contrast to our city's wholesome family values. We were swift in taking a stance against the *Nightfall* book series after it brought the same immorality here. Let's be sure to take the same swift stance against this shop."

The author of the opinion piece went on to paint a picture of their town as an idyllic community of families living in homes with white picket fences. To Edie, and she was sure the entire vampire community, those picket fence posts bore both a literal and metaphorical resemblance to wooden stakes. She thought about the unhoused whose encampments were frequently broken up to maintain that idyllic image, and she knew it wasn't just the vampire community feeling ousted so that the residents could maintain some sick "friendly" facade.

She was steaming when she handed the phone back to Sid.

"A thing of beauty, isn't it?" Sid asked, beaming. "I've got to admit, I was wrong about you. I really thought that you were going to be a Karen yourself when I first met you, but you've quickly become one of my favorite people."

Edie did not share Sid's glee.

"Are people really so narrow-minded that they're going to try to shut down my coffee shop because I put up a portrait of Dracula and added some raspberry syrup 'blood' drops on top of whipped cream for a drink?"

"Relax," Sid said. "Haters are gonna hate, but there's no such thing as bad publicity."

Edie hoped he was right, though her concern was deeper than simply whether or not some suburban keyboard warrior found her coffee shop wholesome enough. Chances were high that the writer of the op-ed had never frequented her coffee shop so it wasn't as though she'd lost a customer. She wasn't scared of the "hater" as Sid had put it. She was scared of the hate. It was the ideas in the article, and the traction behind those ideas, that worried her.

"I'll take a vanilla Draculatte," Sid said. "On the house for your first customer?"

"That'll be $5.25," Edie said.

Sid frowned and fished through his wallet for change. "Tell you what. I'll start a tab. I'm going to be one of your new regulars anyway now that this beauty is working here." He sent a grin Empty's way, and Edie watched as she actually swooned a little at the compliment.

"I'll get your drink, babe," Empty said, and she selected a mug to start making the beverage. Edie was going to have a talk with Empty. She couldn't afford to be giving out freebies all day. If Empty wanted to foot the bill for all of Sid's drinks, then she supposed that was her choice, but Edie would have preferred to see Sid pay for his own lattes.

Finally, the door chimed, and a couple of customers stepped inside. Edie held her breath as the pair of girls looked around, and she released it as they nodded appreciatively at the decor, chuckling together over the new beverage names as they stepped up to the counter.

"What does it mean to add a shot of blood, and why does that cost an addition $4?"

Edie could tell that she had piqued the girls' interest, which was exactly why she'd advertised the blood shot. Penny had promised that the vampires would pay a premium, and if Edie had learned anything about marketing, it was that people would overpay for regular items that appeared special in some way.

Edie pointed to the blood bag labeled O-neg that she'd rigged with a spout and filled with a brown sugar simple syrup that she'd reduced so that it had a thicker consistency than her other syrups and dyed red to have the color and consistency of blood. The blood syrup for the actual vampire beverages was labelled O-pos, and it was kept in a safe, to be brought out only when she and Penny were the only staff working.

Edie didn't give an explanation for the syrup. "You can try it if you dare."

This time real excitement crossed the girls' faces, and they both nodded.

Edie made them their drinks and watched their reactions.

"Oh, that's good," one girl said in surprise.

"How fun," the second added.

They took their beverages to go, talking excitedly as they headed out the door, which Edie hoped meant that they'd tell their friends about her shop.

The relaunch might not have been met with a flood of new customers all pining to try vampiric beverages, but Edie was confident that business would pick up.

Edie was in the middle of making a Transylvanian Fog with

a pump of O-neg when she turned at the sound of the door chime to see Penny step inside, her breath catching in her chest at the sight before her.

Edie had thought Penny pretty the instant they'd met, but dressed for the launch party in the dark purple, lacy gown that perfectly highlighted every curve she was stunning. Edie had to remind herself to focus on the beverage she was making before allowing her gaze to trace slowly across Penny's body, noting the tease of skin beneath the lace sleeves, and landing on the hint of cleavage below the pearl necklace she wore.

"You look . . ." All of Edie's words for the end of that sentence felt too big to speak. Ethereal. Mesmerizing. Dangerously seductive.

Penny laughed, and the warm, light chuckle was such a contrast to her bold appearance that it only amplified those intimidating qualities. "You look . . ." She paused to echo Edie's bumbling sentiment. ". . . yourself."

Edie had worn a relatively simple black dress, and she knew she looked nice enough, but Penny was on a different level. She felt so human in comparison to Penny, whose beauty had a transcendent quality to it.

"This has been fun," Blake interjected, "but since we're all here now, and we're not exactly busy, can we toast or whatever it is you wanted to do so that I can head out for the evening?"

Edie nodded and called Empty, who met them behind the counter along with Sid, who apparently thought himself part of the team. The opening was feeling anticlimactic, and she had no grand ideas for a team celebration, but she felt that they needed to mark the occasion somehow.

"All right, everyone put your hands in and say 'Bloodline' on the count of three."

Edie felt ridiculous counting them in, but when they broke their hands apart with a cheer for the shop—even a lackluster cheer—she felt, for the first time since her parents' death, that she wasn't in this alone.

"I'm going to head out as well," Empty said.

"We've got a hot date and the night to ourselves at home," Sid boasted, and Edie cringed as she immediately began planning how she could sanitize her entire apartment the next day.

Empty giggled and she, Sid, and Blake all headed out, leaving Empty and Penny alone in the shop.

"Slow start?" Penny asked.

"In hindsight, this place *is* still a coffee shop first and foremost. Maybe a sunset start was not the most strategic plan."

Penny laughed, and that laugh brought a smile to Edie's face.

"We just need time to build momentum," Edie continued.

Penny's gaze was full of appreciation and care, but behind that Edie could still sense apprehension. She knew that whatever fears she had about the city's reception to the new shop theme were infinitely amplified for Penny. She didn't want to mention the opinion piece Sid had brought in, though she knew she'd have to discuss it with Penny soon enough.

Instead, she leaned into the tenderness, kissing Penny for a deliciously slow moment.

"Sorry," she said with a grin when she pulled back. "I couldn't help myself."

As much as she would have preferred to keep kissing Penny, she wanted to be ready in case any vampire customers did end up venturing into her shop, so she went to the safe and took out the O-pos blood bag, hanging it next to the fake blood syrup.

"I wouldn't hang much hope with that," Penny said. "I've talked to a few of the vampires that I know in town, and they're

154

all skeptical. We've had to hide for a long time."

"I know," Edie said.

But Penny shook her head. "You think you know, but we've had to hide who we are in order to survive. This place could be important for our community, but don't expect it to be immediately embraced with open arms. It's a risk not just for you and me, but for all of us."

As if on cue, the door opened again, and two men in paramedic uniforms entered the coffee shop.

"You came." Penny's voice was full of surprise, and she stepped up to the counter as Edie's pulse quickened.

"I trust your recommendation," one of the men answered, but while he might have trusted Penny, it was clear that he did not trust Edie as he sized her up with a hard, stern gaze.

Edie swallowed her anxiety and wiped her suddenly sweaty palms on her jeans.

"This is fun," the other paramedic said, studying the menu as he stepped up to the counter. "It's nice there's finally a good late-night coffee option."

He stroked his five o'clock shadow as though it was a beard and said, "I'll have a dark-hearted IV drip coffee."

Edie waited for the signal indicating that he'd need the blood shot, but he simply stood and waited for Edie to ring up his order. Perhaps she'd been wrong about the two men who'd entered. Maybe they were simply friends of Penny's.

The man tapped his credit card, and Penny went to pour him his coffee while Edie took the next order.

The second man, the one who'd first spoke, stepped up to the counter. "I'll try the salted carotid mocha," he said, and his eyes narrowed for a long moment before he cautiously raised two fingers and rested them against his own carotid.

For a moment Edie froze, and then she gave him the total and took payment, allowing Penny to make his drink as well.

Edie wondered if his partner knew that he was working with a vampire, but even as the question sprung to mind, she knew the answer was no. She strongly suspected that she was the only human in the city to know the truth about him.

"You're actually going to have a coffee tonight?" the first paramedic asked his vampire partner. "You never get coffees with us."

What would the young man think if he knew the truth about his colleague? Would they continue to work together amicably, or would the difference be too much? Would the first medic embrace his partner, or react with fear?

Edie knew that the only way vampires would ever be accepted was for people to know about them in the first place and realize that vampires weren't monsters, but rather their family and friends. However, she also knew the risk that coming out of the coffin, so to speak, carried.

The two men took their coffees to one of the tables and settled in before trying their beverages.

The vampire lifted his mug to his nose and inhaled before taking a long, slow sip. Then, he turned to meet Edie's gaze and nodded his approval.

The pace of the night didn't pick up, but Edie refused to let that dampen any of her optimism about the relaunch. They'd had one vampire customer, and that was surely a start to getting the word out. And they'd seen a few new human customers come in to try their beverages.

There was a steady trickle of customers until just after midnight, when the shop emptied, leaving Penny and Edie alone.

"I'm optimistic," Edie began, but then Penny was spinning her so that her back was pressed against the counter, and she was leaning in to kiss her, the air getting knocked from Edie's chest.

From their first kiss, Edie had taken great pleasure in kissing Penny, but after their shared night together, the kiss took on an entirely new level of pleasure. Since that night, they'd been so busy getting the coffee shop ready for its relaunch that they hadn't spent much time alone together, a fact which Edie was suddenly desperate to change.

When Penny stepped back, Edie was left a little dazed and a lot turned on.

"What was that for?" Edie asked.

Emotion was thick in Penny's voice when she answered. "For being you. This place . . . it's everything I've ever wanted but didn't even know how to hope to dream for. Tonight has been overwhelming, but in the best way possible."

Edie was a little surprised at Penny's categorization because had you asked her the evening had been underwhelming, with hardly any customers, either vampire or human.

"I never would have dared to hope that there'd be a place I could frequent where I could be myself," Penny continued. "I know you wanted a steady stream of customers and for the place to be packed with both humans and vampires. But that other vampire that came in earlier, did you see the look on his face when he'd left? He mirrored everything I feel: apprehension, but also hope and awe. And it isn't just a safe place for vampires. Where else has Blake ever really belonged? Or Empty? Sid? This place is important, Edie. What you gave us . . . What you've built . . . It's *everything*."

Edie shrugged off the compliment, but Penny refused to let her dismiss the words.

"Do you know how long I've had to hide who I am?"

Edie didn't know and probably couldn't imagine. But she remembered the year she'd been in the closet and how scared she'd been that somebody would find out about her sexual orientation. She remembered worrying that her friends would abandon her, and that she'd lose everything. She'd spent the year vacillating between anxiety and depression, and she remembered how freeing coming out had been.

Penny had been hiding her true self for decades. However terrifying and freeing coming out had felt to Edie, both of those feelings had to be infinitely amplified for Penny.

Edie thought about the opinion piece that Sid had showed her earlier that evening. The town's nosy busybodies could go to hell as far as Edie was concerned. She felt a little deceitful not telling Penny about the piece, but she didn't want to ruin Penny's joy.

She would worry about the town haters, but this wasn't the time for that. For now, she wanted Penny to have that moment of safety and acceptance.

The haters were going to hate, but surely their overblown opinions would fizzle out as swiftly as they'd flamed up.

Good Old-Fashioned Family Values

For the rest of the week, business was slow. Each night saw a vampire customer or two, and human customers continued to trickle in showing some intrigue with the concept, but Edie was starting to doubt that the shop changes would be enough to save the place.

At least the criticism remained minimal and was mostly wielded behind the safety of a screen. Edie hadn't had to counter any narrow-mindedness in person.

And working with Penny was an added plus. She hadn't been sure how their chemistry would translate to the workplace. It was an odd dynamic to move from newly dating to working together like an old married couple, but somehow it worked. They fell into stride alongside one another with a natural flow.

"You know, when I came in today, Blake was getting ready to go back to my place with Empty so he could further discuss the *Nightfall* series with her. Can you believe the two of them have hit it off so well?"

Penny chuckled. "I can picture that pretty easily. On the

surface, they're very different, but I think they actually have a lot in common."

Edie would never have guessed, but Penny was right. Blake and Empty were both looking for meaning and a place to belong even if they seemed to be looking in very different places.

"Have you read the *Nightfall* series?" Edie asked. "Is it weird that there are book series around vampires that have become so popular?"

"I haven't read it," Penny said, "and I don't intend to. While I'm glad that the 'representation,' if you want to call it that, has shifted away from us being monsters, I'm not sure that being fetishized is much better."

Edie wasn't sure how to respond, so she rested her hand on Penny's in a show of support.

"I've heard whispers around our community that the *Nightfall* series is not actually terrible in terms of representation, though."

"Really?" Edie asked.

Penny nodded. "But like I said, I haven't read it."

The conversation ended there as a woman breezed into the coffee shop, followed by a loud gust of November wind. The woman wore a long, black jacket and black gloves, which she pulled off her hands, revealing slender, perfectly manicured, fingers. She wore a thick scarf around her neck, which occluded her appearance, as did the black, wide-brimmed hat she wore, pulled low so Edie could barely make out her bespeckled eyes. A shock of red hair peeked out from under the hat before being buried, once more, beneath the scarf.

Edie waited for her to approach the counter, but she first took in the shop, walking to the bookshelf to trace her fingers over the spines of the books. She thumbed through a tattered copy of *Nightfall*, and then set it tenderly back into its place. Then she walked to each of the portraits, before circling to the counter.

"Hi, and welcome to Bloodline," Edie greeted. "What can I get for you tonight?"

The woman opened her mouth to speak, but another customer spoke first, approaching the woman with eager enthusiasm.

"Ellora Merriweather?"

The customer who'd approached was a member of the crochet club, and she held a large swath of gray crocheted fabric in her arms, eyes shining with excitement.

Edie watched the almost-imperceptible change in the first woman's demeanor. She exhaled and straightened before turning to the woman and pushing the hat up from her forehead.

"It is I," the woman answered. "And who might I be speaking to?"

As the member of the crochet club stammered her name and gushed over the author, Edie realized she did, in fact, recognize her from the grainy photo she'd seen on the back cover of all of Ellora Merriweather's books she'd come across. She'd assumed the photo to be much older than it obviously was because it was black and white and grainy. She'd also half believed that Ellora Merriweather was the name given to a group of ghost writers and publicists since she'd never known anyone to actually see the author before.

Ellora pulled her gloves back on. "I am pleased to make your acquaintance," she said, though Edie thought her voice sounded falsely sweet. She extended her hand, and the other woman juggled her crochet into the crook of one arm for an eager handshake with the beloved author.

Ellora accepted some final praise from the woman, and when as the woman had returned to her group, she turned to Edie. "I had to see it for myself," she said, loud enough for the others to hear. "The news articles were right. This place is serving hot cups of corruption."

Edie felt her blood run cold at the words. "I assure you, we are only serving coffee," she said, keeping her voice as steady and confident as possible. "The cinnamon buns that we get from the bakery down the road *are* sinfully delicious, but that's as corrupt as we get."

Edie chanced a glance at the crochet club, and she saw the change in demeanor in a few members of the group. They were all regulars in her shop, they'd helped crochet the lace table coverings, and yet Edie could see the dilemma they were wrestling with.

Even passively, Ellora had always had an ability to sway town opinions as the city hung its pride on the image of the wholesome romance novels that had made the city famous. If Ellora provided a public statement . . .

Edie's heart sank.

"I have to say that I cannot condone this depravity," Ellora said.

It didn't matter if she made a further public statement or not. Enough people in the shop had heard what Ellora had to say. Word would travel.

With that, Ellora turned to leave, blowing out the door with a much more bitter wind than she'd blown in with.

Edie stood frozen in place as she tried to digest what had just happened.

"I think that maybe I should leave for the night," Penny said.

"What?" Edie asked. She turned to Penny who was even

paler than usual.

"I'm not feeling well," Penny lied.

Edie could hear the fear in Penny's voice, but she couldn't find any reassurances to offer.

Instead, she moved to kiss Penny goodbye.

Penny didn't kiss her back.

The sun had already risen by the time Blake and Empty arrived to relieve Edie for the day shift, but despite the daylight, she walked directly to Penny's apartment, hoping to be able to talk to her about what had happened.

Penny's garden looked entirely different in the light of day. Without the colorful luminescence of the solar lights, there was no mystical ambiance, only the detritus of a garden that had been beautiful once but was now withered and dead, awaiting the cover of snow. The garden saddened Edie, mostly because she wondered how closely it mirrored her relationship with Penny. Was their relationship beautiful under the cover of darkness, only for the bitter reality to be exposed in the daylight?

She knocked on the door, doubtful that Penny would answer. She was probably asleep already, her way of wasting away the daylight hours until she could return to the world under the safety of night.

Sure enough, there was no answer.

She knocked again.

Silence.

Then Penny's voice from behind the heavy wooden door. "Who's there?"

"It's me."

Edie was met with silence for so long she half believed that Penny had walked away from the door, retreating into her house to avoid any further conversation.

But just before Edie could call out again or walk away, she heard the heavy turn of a deadbolt and Penny said, "Give it a minute for me to go into another room so I don't get exposed to any sunlight, and then you can come on in."

Edie did as instructed, waiting until she was sure it had been long enough before letting herself into Penny's home.

She shut the door behind her.

From inside the home, day was indistinguishable from night, and yet the place had a different feel to it than the last time Edie had been there. Granted, the last time she'd been in Penny's home was under much more pleasurable circumstances.

"The door's shut," Edie called, and Penny stepped into the entryway a moment later.

Penny stood silently in the entryway, her fear a palpable presence between them, and all of Edie's own words caught in her throat. There was no right thing to say. No reassurances she could offer. No apologies. Bloodline hadn't been a mistake, but she couldn't promise everything would work out, either.

"Can I hold you?" Edie asked at last—physical comfort the only thing she could think to offer.

Penny nodded, and Edie wrapped her arms around Penny who softened into the embrace. Edie stroked her back and kissed her head until eventually Penny spoke.

"When I'm with you, everything feels possible. Like, I really can have a place in the world."

Edie pulled Penny tighter. She'd felt the same expansion of possibilities in her own life since meeting Penny. Her coffee shop, which had seemed hopeless, had a new direction, but more than that, Edie's own life had found joy again.

"Maybe this has all been a beautiful dream," Penny said. "Maybe what happened last night was the reality check I needed."

"What happened last night was somebody came in with an overinflated ego and thought themselves important enough to offer an opinion on something that really is none of their business."

"What Merriweather said . . . It was the reminder I needed that what we're doing with the coffee shop, it's dangerous."

"She can say what she wants," Edie argued. "We'll continue to push back against her hate."

Penny shook her head sadly. "You don't understand. I got swept up in hope, but vampires have existed in the shadows for good reason. Some of us have had centuries to learn that humans will only ever see us as monsters."

"You're not a monster," Edie argued. "If I can see that, others will be able to see it as well."

"Usually, I love your optimism," Penny began, "but right now, I need you to listen. The shop can be vampire themed, but it needs to end there."

Edie sighed and said, "Okay." If that was what she needed to do until things settled and Penny felt comfortable, then that's what she'd do, but she hated that Ellora Merriweather could come in with puffed up importance and dictate the direction of her family's coffee shop.

"Let's get some sleep," Edie said. "It was a long night."

Penny nodded, and Edie followed her to the bedroom, curling up behind her. The two lay together in silence.

Neither slept.

165

Not In Our Town

Winter settled over the city as Bloodline entered its second week, and as Edie walked the short distance from her apartment to her coffee shop, she hoped that the dusting of snow represented a clean slate, rather than a burial.

As promised, Ellora Merriweather had released a statement about her coffee shop that had been less than flattering, and business had significantly slowed in the wake of the beloved author's public opinion. Still, she refused to believe that hate could win in the end. They'd removed the O-positive blood syrup and had stopped serving vampire customers, though Edie hoped that was only a temporary change until things settled a little.

The fresh white snow crunched under her feet. The afternoon sun was heavy in the sky. It was a Sunday afternoon, so the city was quiet and still, with no rush hour traffic, no students rushing to and from classes, and everyone else inside.

She passed Hank, shivering on the corner in his worn-out jacket and mittens full of holes, and her heart ached.

"I'm headed to open up the shop," Edie said. "You come by later for coffee and a pastry, okay? You can sit inside and get warm for a while."

Hank smiled at her with gaps in his yellowed teeth. "You do good there."

Edie smiled back and continued on her way. She hoped she did good. Wasn't that the point? That was the root of her passion for the shop, and her passion for coffee. It had always been about community and bringing people together and providing a place for people to feel warm, safe, and cared about.

The bright red droplets in the fresh snow jarred Edie from her thoughts, and she looked up, seeing the dripping red trail leading toward her shop. She quickened her pace, immediately wondering who had been hurt and staring at the blood spatter atop the snow.

The minute she rounded the corner, and her beloved family coffee shop came into view, her heart shattered, as she took in the carnage.

The red hadn't been blood, but it might as well have been. Red paint splashed across the entire front of her shop in giant letters.

"NOT IN OUR TOWN!"

The gruesome statement screamed at her from her shop windows, and Edie tried to swallow back the tears that choked up her throat in a hard lump.

Who would do this?

Even as she asked herself the question, she recognized that there was likely no shortage of possibilities. It was the people who boycotted her Draculattes, who banned the *Nightfall* series, who protested pride parades, made bathrooms unsafe for transgender folks, and disassembled encampments for the unhoused.

It was the whole town with Ellora fucking Merriweather—a meat sack full of hatred dolled up in a stupid hat and flowery scarf—as their mascot.

Rage simmered within her like magma, hot and powerful, but she had nowhere tangible to direct that rage so instead it leaked from her eyes in hot tears that burned trails down her cheeks.

She took a deep breath and wiped her cheeks before pulling out her phone.

Her immediate instinct was to call Penny, but she stopped herself. Even if it didn't completely freak Penny out and Penny wanted to help her, the sun was still up so she wouldn't be able to do anything. There was no point upsetting Penny with the news any sooner than she needed to. She'd find out about the graffiti in a couple of hours once the sun set and she came in for her shift.

Edie went to her contacts and without hesitating pulled up Empty's name and hit call.

"Yeah?" Empty said, answering the call.

"I need your help," Edie said, and she proceeded to explain the situation.

It took only half an hour for Empty to pull up to the curb in Sid's car and step out in front of the shop with a bucket full of cleaning supplies and a large vat of white vinegar.

"Fuckers," Empty said, taking a look at the graffiti for herself.

"Yup," Edie agreed.

Sid climbed out of the driver's seat, and Edie was surprised when the back passenger door opened, and Blake climbed out.

"You're all here?" she asked, tears burning her eyes for a different reason this time.

"Of course," Blake answered. Then he studied the graffiti as well.

Edie felt overwhelmed with gratitude. Since her parents'

death, she'd felt alone in trying to save the shop, but the fact that the three of them had immediately all shown up, no questions asked, meant the world to Edie.

"I expected some degree of moral indignation or push-back," Blake began, "but this seems exaggerated."

On the one hand, that was the understatement of the year, and on the other hand, this was exactly the level of response that Edie should have prepared herself for. It seemed exactly in line with how the town responded to those who didn't fit their conservative values.

"We should be able to heat this vinegar and use it to wipe the paint off both the walls and windows," Empty said. "If not, nail polish remover should do the trick, but we'd need a lot of it."

"How do you know what to do?" Edie asked. She had simply stared at the shop dumbfounded, not sure where to begin with cleanup.

Empty shrugged. "Growing up, my church group used to take on these city cleanup volunteer projects. I've helped clean spray paint off playgrounds and downtown businesses."

Edie blinked at her, always surprised by the things she learned about Empty. "That's amazing," she said.

Empty gave that disheartened shrug again, and Sid spoke up. "Don't be too impressed. That church likes to make it look like they're the good guys, but they're also probably the ones who did this."

Edie reached out and gave Empty's arm a squeeze, hating the fact that Sid was probably right. The two of them had grown up within a tight-knit community that claimed to be taking the moral high road while throwing rocks at those they believed to be on the path "below" them. Empty's parents had kicked her out of their house, after all, while assuaging their guilt by handing her rent money. They cared enough to look like supportive parents from the outside, but not enough to love their daughter for who she was.

Edie would always rather be seen as taking the path of sin if it meant that those around her felt loved and included.

Edie unlocked the shop to heat the vinegar in the microwave, and when she went back outside, Sid, Empty, and Blake had already pulled on gloves, and were ready to work.

Sid was the first to grab a cloth and dip it into the bucket of warm vinegar.

"Those fuckers," Sid said, as he scrubbed at the paint. "They'll rip up every last white picket fence post of theirs to use as a wooden stake, and they will never see that it was their own fear and hate that destroyed their precious community. It will always be our fault for existing outside of their insular world view."

For a moment, Edie watched as Sid scrubbed angrily. It was the first real show of emotion she'd seen from him. She'd only ever seen his bravado and arrogant swagger before. He'd always seemed so cocky.

Empty was silent as she began to scrub at the letters beside Sid.

The two of them had been made to feel unsafe before the vampire personas. They'd always been a little different, and that difference made them a target for no reason other than fear of the unknown. Edie channeled all the rage she felt as she picked up a cloth and began to scrub as well. Empty and Sid deserved to be embraced for their eccentricities, not ostracized. Penny and the other vampires deserved a place to drink coffee.

Bloodline was a harmless gathering place, and she'd be damned if she let the bigots in town scare them back into silence.

As the sun began to set, the already cold temperature

plummeted, and Edie's fingers began to feel numb from the cold wind on her wet hands.

"You're all free to head home," Edie said. "I'll chip away at this a little longer, but we can finish it up in the morning."

None of the three stopped scrubbing at the graffiti.

"You know," Blake began, his gaze focused on the wall as he kept scrubbing with an intense determination. He had been unusually quiet all evening. "I didn't actually graduate last year."

Edie let her cloth fall to the side as she looked over at him. "What?"

He didn't meet her gaze. "I tell everyone I did, because it was my last semester, and I should have graduated. It's embarrassing. I had a couple of core courses that I had to finish up, and some of those numbers courses were not my thing. I really tried, but I couldn't pass them. I'd received a conditional acceptance to the philosophy master's program, but then I failed statistics. I was going to retake it this fall. Your dad was going to tutor me. But then . . ."

"I'm so sorry," Edie said.

"I said before that we're both in a state of morphogenesis, trying to figure out what new paths our lives are going to take. Saving this coffee shop is important to all of us. We aren't leaving."

Edie was so awash with gratitude that she no longer noticed the cold as the night sky shifted from slate gray to a deep black, behind the yellow-orange glow of the city lights.

"What happened?"

Edie turned at the familiar voice, and even in the dim light she could see that Penny was a shade paler than usual.

"Bloodline got tagged," Empty said, saving Edie from having to explain. Edie wasn't sure she'd have been able to form words in the face of the abject fear she saw etched in Penny's delicate features.

"What did it say?" Penny asked.

"It said 'Not in our town,' like we're going to be run off with a paintbrush," Sid said, his bravado returning.

"We're going to get it clean," Edie promised, though she knew that she could scrub off every last bit of the red paint from the windows and the walls, and it wouldn't scrub away Penny's very legitimate worries.

Penny didn't say anything. She picked up a cloth and stepped next to Edie, who got the sense that Penny wasn't simply scrubbing away the letters from the shop but was scrubbing away her own connection to the place.

Edie's hands were red with the paint that leaked from her sponge, and she hoped that at the end of all of this, they weren't going to be red with the blood of anyone she loved. The last thing she wanted to do was endanger any of them.

She was starting to wonder how far the city would go to protect their clean-cut image.

The five of them worked through the night until, at last, the final smears of red paint were scrubbed away from the storefront, and no trace of the graffiti remained.

"Thank you all for your help," Edie said, around chattering teeth. She dropped the sponge from her hand into the bucket, struggling to pull her gloves off as her frozen fingers were stiff and uncoordinated.

Blake, Sid, and Empty said their goodbyes and got back into Empty's car to leave. In lieu of the work they'd done all night, the coffee shop would be closed for the day, and Edie would reopen for her sunset shift.

"You should go get warm," Penny said.

Edie studied Penny, who couldn't meet her gaze, and despite the chill that had penetrated her very core she felt hesitant to leave.

"Maybe I could warm up at your place?" Edie suggested. "We could take a hot shower together?"

Penny found a crack on the sidewalk intensely interesting, and she scuffed at it with the toe of her shoe. "I don't think that would be a good idea," she said.

The crack in the sidewalk suddenly appeared to be a chasm between the two.

"If you want out of Bloodline, you can say so," Edie said. "I know tonight scared you, and I understand if it is all too much for you, but that doesn't have to change anything between us."

This time, Penny did meet her gaze, and the heartbreak Edie saw there was enough to tell her that Penny had made up her mind.

"Humans and vampires shouldn't mix," Penny said. "It was wrong to tell you the truth about me. I endangered myself, I endangered every other vampire, and possibly worst of all I endangered you."

Edie shook her head. "You didn't. I'm not in danger. It was a little paint."

"Sure, it was a little paint," Penny said, "until it's more than a little paint. Until you lose your coffee shop or, worse, your life. And for what? You're not going to single-handedly make the world embrace vampires, after we've been classified as monsters since the dawn of time."

"But you're not a monster," Edie said. "If I can see that, others can as well."

"I'm not?" Penny asked. "You know what vampires do? We get you to let us in and then we bleed you dry. Both literally and metaphorically. If I stay in your life, that's exactly what would happen. You're going to lose everything you care about for this vampire coffee shop. Take down the vampire images, get rid of the books, call your drinks lattes again, not Draculattes, and come up with some cozy seasonal beverage for people to hibernate with. All of this was a mistake."

"Penny," Edie said, reaching for Penny's hand, but she shrugged away from the touch and turned to flee down the dark sidewalk into the final stretch of night.

Edie wiped furiously at the tears that leaked from the corners of her eyes. She refused to fall apart. If there was one thing she'd come to learn, it was that she could pick herself back up. Of all the things she'd been through in the past year, a breakup was not going to be the thing that broke her.

She picked up the bucket of cleaning supplies and let herself into the shop to dump the vinegar down the drain and tuck away the buckets. She looked at all the new decor, the vampire portraits, and the bookshelf of spooky vampire-themed books. She wasn't going to take any of it down.

Penny didn't have to believe in the idea for her to still believe in it. If she got rid of the vampire decor, it was the same as admitting that Penny was right, that her life *was* better off without vampires in it, which Edie wholeheartedly disagreed with. Her life was better with Penny in it. Her life was also better with Empty and Sid in it, and those two hadn't spent their entire night scrubbing paint off the walls for Edie to pander to the people that had made them feel othered.

Edie didn't care if she lost everything. She wasn't going to denounce those she cared about the most.

What was worth fighting for was so much bigger and more important than her family's coffee shop.

What's Brewing?

The days and nights crept by slowly, and Edie grew a little more disheartened with each long, lonely shift she worked. There had been an initial uptick in customers, likely due to sheer curiosity about the shop, but she was disheartened to see that as they settled into normalcy, the customer base was not much higher than before. In fact, Edie would say that there were fewer customers. At first, she'd attributed the midnight hours to the lack of customers she was seeing as she'd never worked full nights before, but Blake reported that the day shifts were slow as well.

She'd tried calling Penny a couple of times since she left, but Penny hadn't answered her phone and never called her back, which told her everything she needed to know. She tried to empathize with Penny and understood her fear, but when she thought about the way Penny had simply cut her out of her life, she had a hard time dispelling the anger.

Edie didn't want or need Penny's protection. She was an adult who'd gone into both their relationship and their business partnership with her eyes open. She'd made the decisions for herself, and she didn't appreciate Penny acting as some martyr, saying that she needed to leave to protect Edie.

175

She could understand why Penny would think that she was being pie-eyed and overly optimistic about the situation. Penny had been living as a vampire for decades, and this was all new information to Edie who'd learned that vampires existed less than two months earlier, but that didn't mean that Edie wasn't capable of doing her own risk analysis.

She'd made the choice. She'd taken the chance.

Edie was seething on her walk home, her anger clinging to the air as it puffed out of her when her phone rang.

For a moment, she thought that maybe it was Penny finally calling her back, and she was crestfallen when she pulled the phone from her pocket only to find an unrecognized number lighting up across her screen. In her disappointment, she almost tucked her phone away, not wanting to deal with her insurance, bank, or electric company, because those were the only phone calls she was receiving lately. But something compelled her to answer anyway.

"Hello?"

"Hello! Is this Edith McLean, owner of Bloodline Coffee, formerly known as the McLean Family Coffee Shop?"

The woman's voice that floated through her phone speaker had a superficial-sounding charm to it, enthusiasm that was dialed about one notch too high to sound authentic. It also sounded vaguely familiar, though Edie couldn't place how she recognized the voice.

"This is she," Edie said, immediately suspicious.

"My name is Janice Cheung . . ."

The words drifted as the recognition of the name and voice hit Edie. Why was their nightly local news anchor calling her?

". . . I wanted to know if you'd be available this afternoon to discuss the recent changes to your family's shop."

Edie held the phone to her ear but said nothing, stunned into silence.

"Edith?"

She wasn't sure what to think, let alone say. She thought about the opinion piece that Sid had shared, and the blog post Ellora Merriweather had written. So far, the press hadn't exactly been in her shop's favor. And yet, Janice continued . . .

"We're so intrigued by the concept of your shop, and we would really like to highlight the place in our local feature."

A spark of hope flickered within Edie.

"You want to highlight Bloodline?" she echoed stupidly.

"We think that you have a very innovative idea, and we'd love to hear more about the inspiration for your revamped coffee shop, pun fully intended."

Edie thought about what could happen if Bloodline were to receive some good press. She didn't harbor any illusions about changing the minds of those who held a fierce hatred for vampires due to misguided moral principles. But what about those who were on the fence. Those who maybe felt a little uncomfortable with the idea, but couldn't quite pinpoint why, and who only needed to see that her coffee shop wasn't going to corrupt anyone or lead to the downfall of the city to realize that their world could be more expansive. Maybe there would be others like Empty and Sid, who were a little alternative, but in need of a place to belong just like everyone else. Maybe, even if the place could be a little more embraced by the city, some of the vampires would start trusting Edie and would venture in for blood-based beverages.

Would Penny come back then? Edie wondered, and she immediately chastised herself for even allowing that hope to flit through her consciousness. Penny had made her choice.

Still, the question remained audible from somewhere deep inside of her, and that question was likely the real reason she answered the way she did. "When and where would you want to meet?"

They scheduled their meeting for 3:00 p.m., outside of Bloodline, and then the call clicked off, leaving Edie to try to gather her thoughts into something coherent. She tried to temper her hopes, but still her thoughts wandered, lazy imaginings of a packed coffee shop, day and night with clean-cut soccer moms drinking Draculattes at a table next to goth young adults, dressed in all black with metal spikes protruding from their ears, eyebrows, noses, and lips. She envisioned vampires drinking coffee together, gathering for the first time after centuries of isolation.

Edie showed up to Bloodline at 2:30, confident and excited, dressed in the same simple black dress she'd worn for the opening. She wanted something that appeared both classy and on theme. She'd added a floral scarf to add a splash of color, and hopefully make her look a little more approachable in case the black dress looked too much like funeral chic.

She'd spent the afternoon practicing what she might say, and she was ready to wax poetic about how much the coffee shop and all its changes meant to her.

"You're dressed nice," Blake said when Edie walked into the coffee shop a few hours before she was scheduled to work.

She filled both him and Empty in on the request for the news interview.

"I don't know if she'll want to talk to either of you, but I guess be prepared just in case," Edie said.

Blake nodded and straightened his shirt as though the reporter and camera crew were going to come through the door right then and there. Edie wasn't sure what he might say if put in front of a camera, and she hoped that they wouldn't ask to talk to him. Not that he'd say the wrong thing. There was no wrong thing really, and she knew he loved the shop. She also knew that sometimes the things he said were a little hard to interpret.

"Are you sure this is a good idea?" Empty asked as she worried at her fingerless gloves while Sid frowned beside her, sipping on a Draculatte that Empty had no doubt covered the cost of.

"Why wouldn't it be?" Edie asked.

Empty shrugged, "I don't know exactly; it just doesn't feel great. You know that moment in Carrie right before they pour pig's blood on her head?"

"This isn't that," Edie said.

"I'm with Empty," Sid said. "I don't know that you should be talking to the media. Trust me when I say that nobody is voting Bloodline for prom queen without ulterior motives."

Edie felt some of the hope extinguish within her, and the smoke that replaced that ember smelled vaguely of fear, but she didn't have a chance to examine that fear because before she knew it Janice Cheung and her camera crew were walking through the front doors.

She was shorter in person, Edie noted, a fact she found jarring, given the larger-than-life presence that she exuded.

"You must be Edith," Janice said, a big, bright smile across her face as she extended her hand to Edie.

"Edie, please call me Edie."

"Edie," Janice echoed, cupping one of Edie's hands in both of hers. It was a gesture that was probably meant to be friendly, but after talking to Empty and Sid, she looked down at her hand and felt as though it was ensnared within Janice's perfectly manicured hands.

"Do you mind if we get some shots of the shop before we go outside for our interview?" Janice asked.

Edie nodded before stammering "Of course."

There's nothing here that would seem incriminating or untoward. Happy people drinking coffee.

"Can you introduce us to your staff?" Janice asked.

"This is Blake," she said. "He's been an invaluable member of this coffee shop for years now. He's practically a part of the family."

Blake nodded cordially and shook Janice's hand.

Then she pulled Empty in with one arm. "And this is Empty. She's new here, but she's very quickly become part of the family as well. I can't imagine this place without her."

Empty didn't smile at the compliment. She looked like she was a turtle trying to retreat into its shell. In fact, she didn't smile or greet Janice in any way.

"And you are?" Janice asked as the cameras panned over to Sid.

"Her boyfriend," Sid said, nodding to Empty but saying nothing else.

His response struck Edie as the weirdest of the three. Sid always had something to say.

"He doesn't work here, but he's part of the family by extension," Edie said.

Janice beamed over at Edie, and there was something in the overly bright smile that struck Edie as fake, but she tried to dismiss the concern. It was just the others getting into her head.

"All right," Janice said once the cameras stopped rolling. "Ready to head outside and we can do this interview?"

She followed Janice outside and let Janice position them in

180

front of the shop door, just below the shop sign.

"We'll stand right here so that everyone can see the name of the place," Janice said, motioning for the camera crew to take their place.

Edie rocked a bit on the heels of her feet, hoping to dispel some of her nervous energy.

This is really happening, Edie thought. Fear was etched into her excitement, but she tried to focus on the excited energy. This could be a really good thing for the shop.

"Are you ready?" Janice asked.

Edie nodded and took a deep breath to steady herself. *I can do this*, she told herself. They were going to be talking about her family's coffee shop. There were few things in the world she cared about more. Her passion would come through, and that was all that mattered. If she could show how much she cared about the place, then others would come to care about the place.

It was a whirlwind of activity as Janice motioned for her camera crew to take their places, and Edie almost thought she detected a hungry gleam in her eyes, but when she turned her smile to Edie, it appeared warm and friendly. Then Janice was giving her the countdown, and Edie tried to focus on herself and looking composed for the camera.

"Hello," Janice began, holding her microphone as she spoke to the camera. "This is Janice Cheung with your Channel 8 News at 8, reporting to you from outside the local coffee shop, Bloodline Coffee. Some of you might remember this shop as local favorite the McLean Family Coffee Shop."

Edie blinked at the categorization of "local favorite." Longtime local coffee shop would have been accurate. The shop existed, yes. It had never been noteworthy, though. Even at the start, it had never been a local favorite.

"I'm here today to talk with the owner, Edie McLean, about the recent changes she's made to her family's shop."

Edie stood a little straighter and smiled at the camera.

"Tell me, Edie, how long have you owned Bloodline Coffee?"

Janice held the microphone out to her, and she took a deep, steadying breath before answering. "Essentially, all my life," Edie said. "I was born into this coffee shop. I grew up here. I spent more time inside of these four walls growing up than I did my own house." She hoped her voice sounded sweet and charming to ease the worries of her critics. "When my parents passed away this past spring, ownership officially transferred to me, but this place has been in my family for generations. My great-grandfather started the shop after coming home from the war, and after everything he'd seen on the battlefield, this place literally saved him."

The town was all about family values, and Edie was going to make sure that the town knew that her family was at the core of her coffee shop. It was started by a veteran, a war hero. How could her shop be more wholesome?

"I'm very sorry to hear about the loss of your parents," Janice said.

"Thank you," Edie answered. "It was very unexpected, and I miss them every day."

Janice took a moment, nodding sympathetically before transitioning the conversation.

"In the past couple of weeks, you've made the choice to rebrand your family's coffee shop. Can you tell me a bit about the decision to turn your shop into a vampire-themed cafe?"

Edie took a moment to find her words and collect herself. She'd prepared for this question. It was, quite literally, the reason she was doing the interview. Still, she felt the pressure. She had one chance to tell her story and change some minds.

"I love this coffee shop more than anyone," Edie said. "As I said, I grew up here. This place has been my home my entire life. And even I could see, when I inherited the place, that it was overdue for a bit of a change. The place was starting to look a bit outdated and worn down."

"But why not just modernize? Why vampires?"

"This place has always tended to cater to a younger crowd, being on the corner of campus, and our evening hours were one of the things that set our shop apart, so I wanted to expand on those strengths and make this place something fun, youthful, and maybe a little edgy."

Janice smiled and nodded. "I would say you've succeeded at those things. Vampires have really come into vogue these days, with a massive pop-culture following thanks to the *Nightfall* series and other popular vampire fiction."

Edie felt the blush color her cheeks, but she was smiling at the compliment. "Thank you. I really wanted to lean into the concept and do something original. I didn't want this place to be another cookie-cutter coffee shop like you find on every corner."

"You have definitely captured originality," Janice agreed.

Edie beamed, already planning the rest of the interview in her mind. She'd tell Janice about how the writer's group had helped her come up with the punny drink names. She'd talk with her about elements of vampire lore that they'd tried to capture in their decor and theming.

"I'm curious," Janice began, and Edie immediately felt the tone of the interview shift with those two words.

A chill ran up her spine.

"Did it concern you at all that the *Nightfall* series is banned from this city after the influx of vampire tourism the series brought here?"

Edie hardened at the question. "It does concern me, yes, that the book series is banned. I haven't personally read the series, but from what I've heard about the books, they're pretty harmless."

"The majority of our city's citizens would disagree with you on that one."

"Just because it is a view held by a majority of the citizens doesn't make it right. It is so easy for people to judge people and things they know nothing about."

"And *you* know about vampires."

The stony look in Janice's eyes raised the hairs on Edie's arms while the words rang accusingly in the air between them. How she managed to maintain her composure, Edie didn't know, but she stood still and straight and said, "I know my coffee shop, and I know that there is nothing dangerous or sinful about the place."

"I've heard you offer blood shots to your beverages," Janice said.

"We do," Edie said, not allowing herself to be shaken by the implication. *She can't know.* "The syrup is a mixture of brown sugar and food coloring. It's designed to look like blood."

Janice laughed, but her laugh sounded inauthentic and put on, and Edie wondered what kind of show Janice was trying to put on for the Channel 8 News at 8.

"I have to say," she said, "everything is themed so convincingly I almost thought you were going to tell me that you've rebranded as a coffee shop for real vampires, and that your blood shots are made of real blood."

She can't know, Edie said to herself again. She hoped that her shock didn't show through, as she tried to put on an amused expression. "That would be something," she said.

"Something indeed," Janice agreed, before shifting her focus back to the camera. "Well, you heard it here, folks. Bloodline Coffee is nothing more than a quirky coffee shop with all sorts of fun theming for you to sink your teeth into."

The cameras cut, and Edie was left standing on the sidewalk dumbfounded, wondering what lead to the change in questioning. What did Janice know?

She can't know about the blood. Penny and I are the only ones who know.

"I think I got what I came for," Janice said as she and her crew finished packing everything up. "Thank you for your time."

Edie nodded numbly and watched as Janice and her crew got into their van and drove away.

She was left with a deeply unsettled feeling. She'd have to watch the news that evening, but even the thought of it caused her chest to clutch with fear.

She can't know.

And yet Edie got the sense that somehow Janice Cheung knew *exactly* what was brewing inside Bloodline Coffee.

The Channel 8 News at 8

The knot in Edie's stomach tightened with each hour that passed. The clock ticked closer to 8:00 p.m. like a doomsday clock ticking down to inevitable destruction. Edie had hoped that the newscast would be a life preserver for Bloodline Coffee, but the interview had extinguished those hopes. She had no idea what Janice knew or what her angle would be, but she knew that she wasn't going to turn on the news tonight and find a happy, friendly depiction of her harmless coffee shop.

Oh no, people would be coming for her with wooden stakes, she was sure.

"Maybe it's not as bad as you think," Empty said. She and Sid had offered to stay to watch the newscast with her, even though Edie had insisted she'd rather watch the carnage alone.

"Maybe," Edie said, though she didn't actually believe that for a second. Empty and Sid didn't know the truth about Bloodline, so they didn't know what was on the line. Edie couldn't tell them even though they were probably going to find out about all of it before the end of the night.

Customers trickled in. A few students sat and drank coffee behind their laptops, and a small group of friends chatted over teas. But, overall, the shop was quieter than ever, if not more so. After Elora Merriweather's unfortunate visit and blog statement about her coffee shop, her business had tanked, and she felt certain that, as dire as things were, they were about to get a lot worse.

Eight o'clock was met with a solid stone of dread that settled into her stomach, heavy and deeply uncomfortable. Edie set up her laptop on the counter to play the news broadcast, and she, Empty, and Sid all gathered around, watching wordlessly, waiting to see what Janice Cheung was going to say about Bloodline.

It was 8:17 when the segment on Bloodline Coffee came on the air. Thankfully, there were no customers at the counter, as her entire focus was on the broadcast from the instant the picture of her shop popped up in the upper left-hand corner of the screen. Janice Cheung, from the safety of the newsroom, sat in the center of the screen and delivered the gut kick of a headline.

"Transfusion tea? Lymphocyte latte? A vampire-themed coffee shop has bitten into our city, but is the shop serving nothing more than spooky puns or is there something more sinister being served up within this shop."

Edie felt her stomach churn with tension, nauseating her with the thought that this broadcast could snuff out the remaining hope for her family's shop.

"The McLean Family Coffee Shop, once a quiet local treasure, has recently been rebranded as Bloodline Coffee, a quirky nighttime coffee shop that hopes to capitalize off of vampire popularity, renaming classic lattes to fit the shop's lore."

Edie watched herself come on the screen, smiling as she spoke. "I wanted to make coffee fun, youthful, and a little edgy."

The camera cut back to the newsroom where Janice talked about vampires saturating the popular media, and how the

Nightfall series had taken over the city "like a virus" before swift regulations had banned the books across town.

"They're really laying it on thick," Sid said. "The busybodies in this town really have nothing better to do."

Edie could tell that he found the news segment amusing, but she couldn't let the negative portrayal roll off her shoulders quite so easily. She felt terror grip her as she dreaded each word.

She was on the screen again, talking about her shop. Smiling and proud and so stupidly naive about the trap she'd been cornered into.

"We offer a 'blood' shot to our drinks," she watched herself say. "The syrup is a mixture of maple syrup and raspberry. It's designed to look like blood."

"Clever theming aside, however," Janice continued from the newsroom, "sources have indicated that perhaps there is more to Bloodline Coffee than initially meets the eye. Could there be *real* blood in the blood shots? You tell me."

She doesn't know anything.

The news segment shifted to the footage of the inside of Bloodline. There was footage of Edie introducing Blake and Empty and Sid.

"He doesn't work here, but he's part of the family by extension."

The segment cut to a TikTok video where Sid held up a glass of blood and took a long, slow sip, licking the red fluid from his lips.

"Foolish mortals," Sid said while his name flashed beneath him: "Sidney 'Obsidian' Whittaker." "I am part of the sanguinarian elite. I am made stronger by the blood of others, becoming less human and closer to the divine with each sip." He took a sip for emphasis. "I won't fear you any longer. You

188

should fear me."

Silence as Sid, on screen, finished drinking the glass of blood that he had in his hands.

"What the fuck is this?" Edie asked, but when she turned to Sid, she immediately regretted the words. He was frozen in place, rigid and paler than usual. Edie softened as she asked, "Sid?"

Sid didn't answer. He looked crestfallen and terrified as the camera cut to an interview with a random woman on the street.

"I think this is an absolute abomination." Janice was now interviewing an older middle-aged woman, who clutched her handbag to her chest as though it was a shield. "This is not the kind of place or people that I want my grandchildren growing up around. Blood lattes? People claiming to be real vampires? What's next? Animals being sacrificed for satanic rituals?"

The newest Ellora Merriweather novel peeked out of the woman's handbag, a fact that made Edie seethe all the more. The city would back Ellora Merriweather come hell or high water. If she started writing about vampires, they'd redecorate city hall to look like Dracula's fucking castle. Edie, meanwhile, couldn't even rename a London Fog a Transylvanian Fog without coming under fire.

The clip cut back to her earlier interview with Janice.

"So, it's not real blood being served in your coffee shop."

"Of course it's not real blood."

Then back to Janice in the newsroom. "There you have it, folks. Bloodline Coffee may merely be inspired by vampire lore, but the shop has been rebranded to cater to a group of individuals who claim to truly be vampires."

Edie closed her laptop in a rage. She was sure that Janice wasn't entirely done talking, but she didn't care to listen to whatever final dig she may have had.

She could hear her anger echo as it rang in her ears, her blood boiling, every cell in her body on fire.

"I need to get home," Sid said. "My parents are going to kill me." He let out a pained groan. "Oh shit," he muttered under his breath. "Shit, shit, shit . . ."

"Sid," Edie began, but he shook his head.

"That was my personal TikTok," Sid said. "I made that video one day while I was angry and hurt and scared. I didn't think it was going to end up on the local news. We should never have gotten involved in this coffee shop idea. People hated us enough as it was. Oh God, my parents are going to kick me out of their basement."

"Sid, I'm sorry," Edie said. She wasn't sure what she was apologizing for, but she felt like somehow this was all her fault. Maybe Penny was right. Maybe starting a coffee shop for vampires was only ever destined to hurt the people she cared about.

She wasn't saving her shop.

She wasn't saving Empty and Sid.

She wasn't saving Penny.

Quite the opposite, in fact.

Over and Outed

The newscast had felt like a bomb detonating, and yet, jarringly, in the aftermath, her quiet coffee shop appeared very much the same as ever.

Empty and Sid had hurried off to do damage control at home, and Edie was left with a handful of customers, drinking beverages and chatting, unaware that her world had been turned on its axis.

Bloodline Coffee didn't serve actual blood-based beverages anymore, and Janice Cheung hadn't landed on the true nature of what they'd tried to build, but her newscast had landed far too close to the truth for comfort.

Penny had been right to shut things down and distance herself from the place. Edie had wanted to create a coffee shop for vampires, and she saw now that not only had it been a failed effort, but it had been a big mistake.

Edie stared vacantly at the portrait of the coffin that had replaced the family photos, and the funeral-black seat cushions that had replaced the dated-but-cheery floral prints. The rebranding hadn't revitalized the place. It had killed it.

Eventually the customers trickled out, leaving the shop

vacant and Edie alone with her thoughts.

Her mind kept flashing to the look on Penny's face the last time she'd seen her. The look on Sid's face. On Empty's. A mix of fear, sadness, and defeat for all three.

Edie cleaned up the shop and then turned the sign to "closed." She had no interest in staying for the rest of her shift. The best she could do was go home, regroup, and figure out how best to help those she cared most about.

She didn't care what happened to her shop.

Edie locked up and walked the short distance back to her apartment, feeling a knot of tension twist within her. She realized that she was nervous to go inside and face Empty. What was she supposed to say?

She hadn't known that Janice Cheung would find Sid's TikTok video to air for that news segment. She hadn't even known that Sid had made such a video, but she couldn't bring herself to deflect the blame she felt. In her mind, she'd been trying to create a space where Empty, Sid, and Penny could all belong, but had she unintentionally exploited them all?

She had known that a vampire coffee shop would make waves in their city, and whether there were noble intentions at the core or not, she'd still rebranded the shop in hopes of making a profit and saving her family's shop.

She found Empty and Sid in the living room, Sid with his head in his hands and Empty sitting beside him rubbing his back.

"It didn't go well," Edie observed.

"I told my parents it wasn't real blood," Sid said, "but they were all 'it doesn't matter if it was real or not, it's the principal behind it' and 'what are our church friends going to think?' I'm not sure if I'm being kicked out or disowned or what. I got out

192

of there pretty quick. Maybe they'll cool down overnight?" He didn't sound hopeful.

"If I'd have known, I would never have spoken to the reporter," Edie said. "I'm so sorry."

"It's not your fault," Empty argued.

Edie shook her head. She'd made a mess of things. There was no denying that.

"I shouldn't have rebranded the coffee shop. I knew the city wouldn't react well. They banned the *Nightfall* book series. People protested a simple Draculatte. I knew how people would react to the shop's changes, and yet I decided to make a statement in a last-ditch effort to save my shop. All it has done is hurt everyone I care about."

"Your coffee shop is the first place I've ever felt truly welcome," Empty said. "Don't you dare apologize for it."

"You tried to warn me about doing the news interview, but I was so determined to get the shop some press."

"Edie, stop," Empty begged. "Don't let the haters win. This city needs your coffee shop more than ever."

Edie sighed. Even if she could think that she was doing the right thing and somehow forgive herself for the fallout, she wasn't sure she could muster any belief that her business could be saved.

Bloodline was wounded and, try as she might to fix things, she was fairly certain the place was bleeding out.

Shattered

It had taken Edie forever to fall asleep, and the sleep that she had achieved had been fitful and broken. She assumed her frequent wakeups were from bad dreams, though she couldn't recall any specifics. All she knew was that she kept waking with a pit of dread in her stomach and a heavy stone of guilt.

When her phone rang, she half expected the sound to be one of those dreams, but as consciousness began to pull the sleep from her eyes, she realized that the ringing of her phone was very much grounded in reality.

Edie frowned and turned over in bed, reaching for the phone, which was plugged into a charger on her nightstand. The frowned turned to worry when she saw Blake's name across the screen.

"Hello?"

"I need you to come by Bloodline," Blake said. Edie could hear the shaking in his voice, and she knew that whatever was going on, it wasn't good.

"I'm on my way," Edie said. She didn't bother asking more questions. She didn't even give Blake a chance to tell her what was going on. She simply got dressed as quickly as she could and rushed over to the shop.

She practically sprinted the couple of blocks to the shop. As she ran, she played through every possible scenario she could think of. They ran the gamut from the harmless "Blake forgot his keys," to the terrifying "someone is seriously hurt." She wished she'd given Blake a chance to explain.

She rounded the corner and her family's pride and joy came into view, stopping her short. She saw her dreams shattered alongside the front window, thousands of fragments littering the snow-covered sidewalk.

"The police are on their way," Blake said, but Edie only distantly heard the words.

She spent a fraction of a second trying to calculate the cost of a replacement window, immediately recognizing that a repair or replacement would be impossibly out of her budget. The insurance she'd had to cancel would have come in handy, but it was too late to dwell on that.

Tears burned her eyes, but Edie refused to let them fall. She went to the front door and stepped inside, though she could have easily gone through the gaping hole where the window once was. When she found the front door unlocked, her stomach dropped, and she realized that there would be more damage than the broken window.

At first she'd assumed someone, angry at the shop's new concept, had simply thrown a brick through the window, but someone had entered her shop through the window and let themselves out through the front door.

Dread clutched at Edie as she turned the doorknob and stepped inside. She went first to the register. She didn't keep much money in there, but every cent mattered to her. Her relief at finding the register still locked was fleeting and quickly replaced with panic at what else the intruder or intruders might have taken.

Nothing appeared stolen. Her mugs were all in their places, the espresso machine appeared untouched, and her fridge remained stocked.

Maybe someone had come in looking for the blood, only to find none there, and so they'd let themselves out.

Edie comforted herself with that idea.

It was then that Edie noticed the door to the back room ever-so-slightly ajar.

She'd never fully understood how someone's blood could run cold until that moment. As she walked toward the back room, she felt her stomach rise to her throat, the same way it would when dropping from the top of a roller coaster. She didn't know what she was going to find on the other side, but she knew in her bones that her family's legacy was dead on the other side.

She pushed through the back door and let out a strangled cry. The room smelled of smoke, and she immediately pinpointed the source. Her family's brand-new twenty-five-kilo roaster, the one that was nearly bankrupting her, that her parents had spent everything on, had a piece of lumber jammed into the roasting bowl.

Edie's feet carried her toward the invaluable piece of equipment, even though her whole body felt numb. The metal paddles for stirring the beans were bent around the thick piece of wood. Wood chips had been poured into the grinder, jamming it up. The machine would never run again.

"Not in our town."

The same words that had been spray-painted across the storefront were now spray-painted in cheery blue letters across the back wall. The bright color mocked her grief.

She could call the police, but even if they caught and charged the culprit, which Edie didn't even think they'd be motivated to put effort into, the roaster would never work again. She'd never be able to pay back her debts. Everything she'd worked for was over.

Edie sank to the floor, leaning against the wall, wishing she could cry or scream or feel anything. All she felt was dead inside. Dead like her family and their coffee shop and their dreams.

So Tragically Mortal

Edie knew all about loss. She'd been standing atop Machu Picchu, about to take a selfie, when her cell phone had buzzed in her hand, and she'd answered her phone to the news that both of her parents were dead. She'd gone from the absolute best moment of her life to the absolute worst in less than a minute.

Still, losing the McLean family's coffee shop, even if it was no longer called The McLean Family Coffee Shop, hit hard. Her family's legacy had landed on her shoulders, and it hadn't even survived the year.

Edie slept the day away or, rather, tossed and turned in bed, wishing that sleep would offer a reprieve from all the guilt and grief she felt. She'd have stayed in bed all day, if her stomach hadn't demanded she eat something, and so she dragged herself to the kitchen, hoping that if she answered her stomach's demands, she'd be able to finally succumb to sleep.

Of course, even in the middle of the afternoon, she found Empty and Sid snacking at her dining room table. She didn't know why she'd have expected otherwise, given that Empty was now out of work. At least Sid, thankfully, had clothes on while he munched on his bowl of Corn Pops.

"'Sup Edie, how's it going?" Sid asked around a mouthful of his cereal.

"Never better," Edie bit back, rolling her eyes as she went to the fridge to see what she could eat.

"When should I expect to be back at work?" Empty asked.

Edie turned and saw the fear and confusion in her roommate's eyes, and she couldn't bring herself to be annoyed by Empty's naiveté.

"I'm sorry, Empty," Edie said. "I have no way to pay for the damages. I had no money to keep the place afloat in the first place."

"You can't close," Empty said, and Edie was surprised at the depth of emotion she saw painted across her roommate's face. Empty's sadness was another dagger to Edie's heart.

"Believe me when I say it's the last thing I want to do, but I'm out of options."

"Our boring-ass town needs that coffee shop," Empty pleaded. "*I* need that coffee shop."

"She's right," Sid said, seeming entirely unaffected by the conversation.

"Look," Edie said, "nobody loved and needed that place more than I did. If I could save it, I would. There's just no way."

Empty paced the kitchen, running her hands through her jet-black hair while shaking her head. She'd go through the same cycle of grief that Edie had before landing on acceptance that Bloodline would have to close.

Edie closed the fridge, having not selected anything, suddenly not as hungry as she was. She took a seat at the table, not having any words of comfort to offer.

"We could try crowdfunding," Empty offered, her eyes brightening as though she'd come up with a genius plan.

"The city hates the place," Edie pointed out. "That's why we're in this boat in the first place. If people cared enough about my coffee shop to try to keep it afloat, they'd have been visiting regularly for coffee. The fact of the matter is that I could beg and plead and appeal to the city for mercy, but we won't get any more than what the three of us would put in."

"Sorry, I'm all out of cash," Sid said, as though unaware of what he was chiming in about, only having heard that he might have to contribute to something.

Edie gave Empty a hard look, Sid only proving her point about the futility of crowd-sourcing funds.

Empty's eyes burned with anger and indignation. "We have to try."

Edie shook her head.

"Why are you giving up like this?" Empty asked, her voice breaking. Edie had to ignore the mirrored emotion that Empty's hurt inspired.

"I'm not giving up," Edie said. "I'm admitting that the battle has already been lost. Bloodline is dead. It's a corpse. It's not coming back."

Silence followed, marred only by the sound of Sid crunching on his cereal. He was the one that broke the silence. "Isn't that kind of the point of this whole thing, though?"

Edie turned to face him. "What?"

He shrugged. "Bloodline is a coffee shop for vampires. Beings that can't be killed. Immortality."

Edie stared blankly, not sure how to respond to his words. Sid didn't understand. He lived in a fantasy world. Vampires may have been real, but Sid's understanding of them was as make-believe as ever.

Her anger quickly morphed into embarrassment at the idea

that she was guilty of the exact same thing because Sid was right: wasn't that the appeal of vampires, after all? She'd learned the truth about Penny, and all of a sudden, she'd thought that if she 'vampified' her coffee shop that it wouldn't die. But it still had.

"Maybe I have my head in the clouds," Empty interjected, "but if I've learned one thing from all of the stories I've read, it's that it's worth fighting to save what you love."

Edie thought back to Penny's anger at having been turned in order to be kept alive. Exactly what she'd done to the McLean Family Coffee Shop. "And I've learned you need to know when to let go."

She turned and left the room before Empty and Sid could say any more. She wanted to save her shop, she did, but she also didn't want to be like Empty and Sid, believing in a fantasy world to create the illusion that things would be okay.

When she got back to her room, her phone rang. She let it ring three times, debating whether she had the energy for conversation before she hit the answer button out of pure curiosity.

"Hello?"

"Is this Edith McLean?" a deep male voice asked from the other end of the line.

"This is she."

The police officer who had taken her statement when she reported the break-in reintroduced himself, and Edie listened blankly as he rattled off the details of his investigation.

"We don't have any leads ... Not much we can do ... Closing the file ..."

None of it really mattered. Without insurance, even if they caught the vandal, her shop would still close.

"There is one thing that's bothering me," the officer said,

almost as though he was still trying to work out the puzzle for himself. "We did manage to view the security footage from the shop across the street, and it shows your storefront perfectly. We can see a couple of people enter your shop with spray paint after the window is smashed, though unfortunately we can't make out any details. But I can't figure out how the window gets smashed in the first place. There's nobody on camera throwing the brick. It just materializes in the air and then flies at the window."

Edie felt her stomach drop.

"Maybe the perp was off camera while throwing the brick and the footage glitched and looped or something afterward. I don't know. Very strange. Still, I've got nothing to go on."

Edie thanked the officer for his time, feeling numb and nauseated. She hung up the phone and sank to the bed.

NOT IN OUR TOWN.

The message had sounded so menacing. Somebody wanted to keep vampires out and had gone to great lengths to do so. Penny was scared for her life because of what that message meant.

But it hadn't been written by some close-minded citizen who wanted to believe the city could remain pure and wholesome if it weren't for Edie's sinful little coffee shop. At least not solely.

A vampire had been involved. Likely one who wanted Bloodline closed out of fear of exposure.

NOT IN OUR TOWN. Not us. You're not going to expose us.

A vampire who wanted to keep every coffin in the city sealed tight.

Somehow, knowing the real reason her shop had been destroyed, made Edie feel worse about everything.

Sid and Empty both spoke of vampires being strong, unafraid, and immortal. If that was true, Bloodline would remain open, and Penny wouldn't have left.

Vampires may not have been vulnerable to aging, but as it turned out, they weren't without their vulnerabilities.

They were still so tragically mortal.

The Living, The Dead, and the Living Dead

The coffee roaster had stopped roasting, as though it was the heart of Bloodline and it had stopped beating. The silence in the roasting room was as shrill and steady as the sound of an EKG machine flatlining. Edie stood vigil over the corpse of her family's dream for a long moment before she was able to bring herself to start taking the photos off the walls.

She'd brought a stack of boxes, and she planned to clear out all the items she was keeping and try to sell the rest for whatever pennies she could get.

She pulled down the photo of her holding the first latte she'd ever made foam art on top of. She was grinning wide, one oversized adult front tooth next to a gap where the second had not yet grown in. The heart she'd made on top of the latte was a little uneven, not nearly perfect to her standards, but easily rivaling the foam art atop drinks in the average coffee shop. She'd perfected latte art at the same age her peers were learning cursive. Coffee was all she knew. The majority of her social studies knowledge came from learning the history of coffee, where it was grown, and how international fair trade worked.

She set the photo in the box and moved onto the next one.

Her as a baby, strapped to her mom's chest, while her mom stood in front of the espresso maker with a mug, smiling. She'd been working in Bloodline since before she could roll over.

"It's in our blood, Edie." Her dad's voice echoed in her mind with each photo she pulled off the wall. She may have inherited a financial mess, but she felt the guilt of the coffee shop's closing landing solely on her shoulders. She had taken a risk to try to save the place, and the risk had massively backfired.

As it turns out, she had inherited every bit of the bad business sense that was in her family's blood.

One by one, the photos came down, and Edie spent time absorbing and reflecting upon all the memories, as though it were a slide show at a funeral. Once the walls were bare, she whispered a soft "goodbye" and headed back to the front of the shop, ready to go home and leave the rest for the next day. She didn't have it in her to box up one more item.

She was surprised to find Empty, Sid, and Blake all sitting at one of the tables.

"What are you three doing here?" she asked. She hadn't heard anyone enter, but she'd been so lost in memory and emotion that the outside world had all but ceased to exist.

"We're going to save Bloodline," Empty announced.

Edie exhaled in frustration. "Please, Empty, we've been over this . . ."

"You haven't even let us try!" Empty argued. "Let us help."

"Do you have a hidden fortune that you're willing to donate?" Edie asked, her hurt morphing into anger.

"No but—"

"Then you can't help," Edie snapped. "Let it rest in peace."

"The news should be airing right about now," Blake said. "I have an inclination that you might be intrigued by what you hear discussed during this hourly episode."

Edie narrowed her eyes even as Empty passed her the cell phone that was airing the nightly newscast.

"What did you do?" Edie asked while a national news story about politics aired.

"Just keep watching," Empty insisted.

Edie waited quiet and curious until she saw a shot of the front of her coffee shop appear on the screen. The smashed window was boarded up, making the place look like a complete dive.

"After being the victim of vandals, some people are rallying behind the Bloodline coffee shop to help save their beloved hangout."

The camera cut to Empty, and Edie felt her jaw drop at the sight. Her roommate was standing in front of the coffee shop, presumably sometime earlier that day, with a reporter interviewing her about Bloodline.

"There are not many places that I've ever fit in, and Bloodline was the one place I've felt truly at home in this town. I haven't worked there for very long, just since the renovations, but I can't imagine my life without the place. Edie, the owner, has really worked to cultivate an inclusive atmosphere. One that is sadly all too rare still and that shouldn't be taken for granted."

Edie felt tears well in her eyes.

"It's a really harmless coffee shop." The camera cut to Sid next, wearing all black, with a trench coat, gloves, and an inverted cross necklace, and Edie wasn't sure how seriously anyone would take him, but she smiled at him, touched to know he'd tried.

"I know people think that there's all sorts of weird and

sinister stuff going on," Sid continued, "but it's really just a coffee shop with some vampire decor. It's all very commercial and all in good fun. Nobody is practicing bloodletting in the back room. I know everyone was up in arms after that video of me was leaked, but that was something I did on my own for a bit of fun. It's all make-believe, this vampire gig of mine, and believe me, it's not the kind of make-believe that's going on here. Edie McLean may act edgy with this whole vampire coffee shop thing, but she's as basic as anyone else."

"I'm sorry that video of yours got you wrapped up in this whole mess," Edie said.

"We're good," Sid promised.

"I have been working at the McLean Family Coffee Shop—Bloodline—for years." Blake had joined the news segment as well. "I was really drawn to the shop's focus on quality, both of coffee and of conversation. Coffee shops these days are a dime a dozen, and each one is the same. They serve the same drinks, have the same ambience, and serve the same clientele. Bloodline tried to be different."

Edie glanced over at Blake, her vision blurry from the tears.

"When Edie first told me that she was going to create a vampire-themed coffee shop, I thought it was gimmicky and uninspired, but I've found the shop to be on an intellectually superior wavelength to any other places in the city. I can understand why most people don't 'get' the concept, but it would be a tragedy to lose Bloodline."

Did Blake essentially insult the intelligence of everyone else in the city? Edie shook her head and wiped at her tears as she chuckled. Her people were rallying behind her. It wouldn't save her shop, but it mattered to her on a very personal level. It might not save her coffee shop, but she'd always remember her friends' words. They'd essentially given Bloodline the very best eulogy.

"Now we go live to—"

Edie handed the phone back to Empty. "I really appreciate the effort that the three of you have put into this place," she said.

"We can save your shop," Empty said, still full of her naive optimism. "We've started a GoFundMe and I have no doubt that we're going to see a whole bunch of donations come through after our news broadcast."

"Let's just call it a night," Edie argued. "I'm done packing things up for today. Why don't I make all of us one last Draculatte and tomorrow we can reevaluate."

It was clear that Empty was disappointed by Edie's lack of enthusiasm, but she nodded, knowing that was the best offer she was going to get.

Edie turned on the espresso maker and pulled four mugs down from the shelves. Making lattes was like a well-choreographed dance, and she moved through each step with grace and ease. Pump the syrup, grind the beans, tamp the grounds, pull the shot, froth the milk . . . Edie moved through each action with a certain reverie. She knew she would still make coffee, whether she went to work at another shop or made lattes for her friends from home, but it would never be the same.

She was finishing the last of the lattes when she heard the sound of car doors slamming shut outside her shop, and all of the sudden fists were pounding on her door and voices were calling in to her.

"Edith McLean?"

"We'd like a moment of your time."

"This is Channel 6 News."

"It's Janice Cheung with the Channel 8 News at 8."

"Channel 4. Could I interview you?"

"Just a few words?"

Edie felt her heart hammer in her chest as she tried to process the sudden rush of press. She didn't know if she should feel excited or terrified. She felt a bit of each and stood in shock, staring at the door while the assault on it continued.

"I knew it," Empty said, beaming. "Our interviews had an impact!"

Edie didn't really believe that. As much as she loved and was grateful for her friends, they'd hardly been the convincing street team they thought they were, and yet the media had come. In droves from the sounds of it.

Tentatively, she moved toward the door and pulled it open. The minute she did, cameras and microphones were in her face and questions were being shouted at her from all directions.

"Are you Edith McLean?"

"How long have you owned Bloodline?"

"Weren't you scared?"

"What are they really like?"

"Are there lots?"

The questions didn't make sense, and Edie's head spun, and then she heard the question that made sense of the questions but made the whole situation all the more confusing.

"When did you find out that vampires are real?"

Edie didn't know how to respond, so she shut the door and looked to her friends. Blake and Empty appeared as confused as she was.

"I knew I'd be taken seriously one of these days," Sid said.

Edie pulled out her phone, which was on silent, and saw over a hundred notifications: emails, missed calls, texts . . . It appeared to be various versions of the questions the media had peppered her with, except that numerous messages also included a link to a video, which Edie opened, hands sweaty.

"I worked at Bloodline for a few weeks. Since it was relaunched as Bloodline." Penny's voice was clear and familiar, but Penny wasn't on the screen. Penny couldn't be seen on camera, so why was she doing a news interview?

Edie's head was a storm of questions and emotions: relief, confusion, happiness, and fear all swirling together to create a tornado inside of her.

"You worked as a nurse previously, correct?" the reporter asked. She had her microphone extended toward what appeared to be an empty chair. "What made you want to leave that career to work in a coffee shop?"

The cacophony outside the shop faded away as Edie gazed dumbfounded at her phone, her mind spinning as it tried to keep up with what was going on.

"I really believed in the changes Edie was making," Penny answered.

Penny's voice was so clear that Edie could practically see her in the chair in front of the reporter as she talked about how she'd met Edie, the quality of the coffee, and how she'd valued Edie's work ethic and creativity.

Edie felt her chest tighten at Penny's words. She had thought she'd never hear Penny's voice again, and now to not only hear Penny, but to hear how much she cared . . . a lump formed in her throat. She felt as though it was herself and Penny in the room, not her and Blake and Empty and Sid, inside of an otherwise Empty coffee shop, looking in on an interview with Penny where she wasn't even on screen.

"When Edie told me that she wanted to rebrand her coffee shop as a coffee shop for vampires, I was probably more skeptical than anyone else. I worried about what the public perception would be. People have an idea about what vampires are, you know? People think vampires are monsters and nothing more."

The reporter leveled Penny with a serious gaze. "You're talking about vampires as if they're real."

Panic rose within Edie as she realized what Penny was doing. She wanted to reach through her phone to tell Penny to stop, to tell her that she didn't have to do this, but she knew it was too late. She was watching a playback. The word was already out.

"What if they are?" Penny asked.

"I watched the interview with the young man who claimed to be a vampire," the reporter began.

"I'm not talking about a goth subculture," Penny stated. "I'm talking about real vampires, living their lives quietly in the shadows."

The reporter shifted in her seat, seemingly uncomfortable with the direction the conversation was heading.

"You're talking as though vampires are living peacefully among us, and this hasn't all been a fun bit of make-believe."

"Vampires are real," Penny stated. Edie's breath caught in her chest at the words. "I can prove it."

The reporter gave a nervous laugh. "That's quite the claim."

"Play back your recording," Penny said. "It will be like I'm not there at all. Vampires' images can't be captured."

"That's ludicrous," the reporter answered, but the interview cut out, and when the camera came back on, the reporter looked pale as a ghost, and she waved the cameras off as she tried to process the information.

The video ended.

Edie set down her phone, her awareness returning to her current surroundings, while a million questions ran through her mind.

What am I supposed to say? How are people going to react? Is Penny okay?

Her mind spun in a million different directions, but one thought came to her, loud and clear over all the others. Penny had done this for her.

Edie pushed her chair back, ignoring the questions that Empty peppered her with, ignoring Blake's philosophical speculation, and ignoring Sid's egocentric comments.

She walked back to the front and opened the door.

Once again, questions started flying her way, but this time, instead of panicking or feeling overwhelmed, Edie felt empowered.

"Yes, I found out that vampires are real, and yes I created a coffee shop that would cater to them."

Follow up questions sounded from every angle. Edie didn't care about the specific questions. She cared that the reporters captured the singular truth of the situation.

"Vampires are not a danger, and just like anyone else, they deserve a place to get a latte."

Creatures of the Night

Edie thought the questions would never end. A crowd had formed around the reporters and camera crews, and Edie began to wonder how she was going to extricate herself from the media circus in order to get home. However, as the sun began to set, the crowd dispersed, almost as quickly as it had arrived. One news van left, and the others sped off after it. Edie pictured them all racing back to their respective studios to review their footage, each hoping to be the first to air the breaking news. Then Edie watched as the crowd of onlookers all stared at her coffee shop, then began murmuring and pointing to the sunset, and they all quickly retreated as well.

Good, Edie thought. *Let them be a little scared right now.* The last thing she needed was a mob of people with all sorts of feelings about vampires, directing those feelings toward her. Let them hide out until morning.

Edie stepped back into her coffee shop and turned to her friends who sat there with unreadable expressions on their faces.

"They're real?" Empty asked in the silence that followed.

Edie nodded, watching the emotions play across Empty's face as she grappled with that information.

"You never told me," she said, her voice small and sad.

"I couldn't tell you," Edie said. "It wasn't that I didn't want you to know, it just . . . it wasn't my secret to share."

"You knew they were real, and you let me keep playing make-believe."

Edie could understand why Empty might have felt a little duped, but she wasn't sure how else she could have handled the situation.

"This doesn't make us any less real," Sid interjected. His voice held an artificially inflated boastfulness that betrayed his own insecurity. If his identity was no longer unique or edgy, what did that make him? It was something both he and Empty would have to grapple with.

"Edie, could I get Penny's number from you?" Blake asked. "I would love to speak with her about this revelation. I must say, it really shakes my understanding of the world. I'd always thought it was a mere metaphorical truth that was the inspiration for vampire stories. If these stories, however, came from a nugget of physiological truth, then I am curious what other stories I need to stop conceptualizing as fiction."

"I'll ask Penny if she'd be up for calling you," Edie said, not intending to do any such thing. She knew without asking that Blake would have been the last person that Penny wanted to talk vampirism with.

Edie hoped that she would get the chance to talk with Penny. She had thought that everything between them was over, but the news interview had Edie questioning things. Did it mean that Penny still wanted to be in her life? Was it her way of bridging the distance between them?

It seemed like forever before Blake, Sid, and Empty all packed up and left Bloodline, all still talking about vampires on their way out, giving Edie a moment of quiet to process everything that had happened and to attempt to gain some clarity.

She debated whether she should go to Penny. They hadn't ended things on the best of terms, and she wasn't sure if Penny wanted to see her, but then again, it was Penny who had essentially outed herself on television in support of Edie's coffee shop.

She was going back and forth when she heard a knock at the door of her coffee shop. She turned, ready to tell off whatever reporter had come around this time, but stilled when she saw Penny standing in the glow of the streetlight outside the door.

Edie's breath caught in her chest. Penny's hair was down, falling in loose brown curls over her shoulders, and Edie's fingers itched to tangle in those curls while she kissed the slender curve where Penny's neck and shoulders met. The pull of attraction was more acute than ever, which annoyed Edie, because she had complicated feelings to unravel.

It wasn't until she saw Penny's mouth make the words "Invite me in?" that Edie thought to move to unlock the front door.

"Come on in," Edie said, moving aside to let Penny pass and then locking the door behind the two of them because it had been a wild night, and she didn't want to deal with anyone else.

For a moment, Edie's gaze locked with Penny, and she saw the war of emotions play across Penny's face: fear, regret, desire, care, sadness.

Then Penny spoke. "How wild did things get?"

Edie's thoughts flashed to the news crews and the crowd all descending upon her en masse. "Pretty wild."

"How did they seem? Did people seem open to everything? Were they outraged? How scared do I need to be?"

Edie shook her head because she couldn't answer that question. She gave the only answer she could. "They had a lot of questions."

Penny bit the inside of her lip as she chewed over her options. "Nobody saw me. I couldn't be captured on camera. So, people don't know what I look like. I have that going for me at least. I probably shouldn't be here. This is the one place they could link me to."

"Slow down," Edie said, but she thought about her broken roaster and suddenly she didn't feel safe in the coffee shop either. Would anyone, in their fear and outrage, come to target them?

"Why did you do it?" Edie asked. "The interview."

"I'd lost everything," Penny said, and the look of sadness in her eyes and the heaviness of it in her voice shattered Edie. "My favorite place. My sense of safety. *You.* Having to uproot my life and start all over again felt so futile if I didn't make some change first."

"I'm sorry I got you involved in all of this," Edie said. "I thought that I could make things better for both of us, but I let my vision for the coffee shop get in the way of hearing your fears. I should have listened to you. We could have been us without all of this external pressure and fear."

"Please don't be sorry," Penny argued. "Whatever happens, I don't regret anything that happened between us for one second. Everything with the coffee shop was to make the world a better place and safer for me and others like me. I could never hold that against you. In fact, it's one of the reasons I love you."

Edie stilled at the words.

"You love me?" she asked. Everything else felt like static behind that.

Penny nodded. "Of course I love you. I fell in love with you the moment I met you, and I've only fallen harder every day since."

Edie reached out and touched her fingertips to Penny's cheek. She could see in Penny's eyes how earnestly she meant the words, and she held Penny's gaze so that Penny could see the same earnestness in her response. "I love you, too."

And then Penny's lips were on hers, and the hurt and chaos and worries all faded away. For a perfect moment, nothing existed besides the two of them.

When they broke apart, it took a moment for Edie to catch her breath and ask the question she knew they were both wondering.

"What happens next?"

Merriweathering the Storm

Edie awoke to the ringing of her phone. In the perpetual darkness of Penny's room, she had no immediate sense of time, and she untangled herself from Penny's arms, reaching for her phone to silence it. Empty's name flashed across the screen, but she swiped left to cancel the call. Then, she checked the time. Nearly noon. Not that time mattered. She pulled Penny's arms back around herself, physically and emotionally exhausted.

She was about to drift back to sleep when her phone rang again.

Behind her Penny stirred, but didn't wake.

Edie grumbled and reluctantly pulled the phone to her, hitting answer, and sternly whispered, "I'm sleeping."

"I'm sorry," Empty said, "but I really need to talk to you."

"Give me a minute," Edie said with a groan, and she extricated herself from the bed carefully so as not to wake Penny. She quickly pulled on her sweatshirt and jeans, and then slipped out of the bedroom to take the call.

"All right," Edie said once she was seated on the sofa in the living room. "What's so urgent?"

"I'm sending you a link," Empty said. "Check your messages."

Edie's phone dinged a moment later, and she pulled the phone away from her ear to open the link that Empty had forwarded to her. When she saw it was the GoFundMe that had been set up for Bloodline, she almost tossed her phone in anger.

"Empty, what are you doing? We don't need a GoFundMe. Bloodline is done."

"Would you set your pride aside for a moment and look?" Empty asked.

Edie was about to argue some more when she caught a glimpse of the number at the top of the screen. All words died in her throat. She was fairly certain her brain had short-circuited. She stopped breathing.

"Edie?" Empty asked after a long moment.

"What is this?" Edie stared at the monetary amount, but the number simply didn't compute for her.

"We've been getting donations all day," Empty answered. "They just keep coming.

Edie refreshed the link, sure that the number was a mistake. When the browser refreshed, the number was higher than before.

"I don't understand."

"Scroll down," Empty instructed.

Edie scrolled. *So many donations.* $20 here, $75 there . . .

"How are there so many?"

"Keep scrolling."

The donations seemed endless, a blur as she scrolled past them all. She almost missed the one that Empty was surely waiting for her to find. At first, it blended in with the other donations, but the—*the zeroes*—Edie scrolled back and blinked at the amount.

"Holt shit," she said, trying to process both the number and the name beside the donation.

"Ellora Merriweather?" Edie managed. "Are we supposed to believe our town's elusive claim to game, everyone's favorite wholesome romance novelist, came out of the woodwork to donate half a million dollars to my family's coffee shop after publicly decrying my shop less than a month ago?"

"It looks that way," Empty said. "And right after her donation, all of the other donations started pouring in. This is enough to reopen Bloodline, right?"

"Um yes," Edie stammered. "This is enough."

She gaped at her phone, scrambling to try to make sense of everything. She'd heard the scorn in Merriweather's voice when she'd previously denounced the shop. She'd fueled the hatred that had destroyed her family's business.

"It can't be her," Edie said. "Somebody else must have used her name."

"Somebody else with half a million dollars to invest in a coffee shop?" Empty asked. "I suppose it could be anyone really."

"You're a brat," Edie said.

Empty laughed, and the sound was so light and jovial that it cracked through the defenses Edie had. She didn't understand the donations, but there they were. Enough money to buy a new roaster. Fix the shop. Pay off all her debt. Reopen.

"Bloodline isn't going to have to close?" Edie asked, tears forming in her eyes.

"Some things are hard to kill," Empty answered.

Edie blew out a breath and swallowed back the tears. "Thank you," she said, wishing that she could give Empty a big hug.

"Your coffee shop means a lot to people," Empty answered. "Go call the bank. Get a new espresso machine with a working steamer. Maybe order some spooky goblets to serve the beverages in. Let's do this."

Edie nodded, already forming the to-do list in her mind.

This was her second chance, and she wasn't about to squander it.

She ended the call but kept her phone in her lap, staring down at it in wonder.

Ellora Merriweather? Really? Of all people.

She heard the bedroom door open, and she turned as Penny stepped out into the living room.

"That was Empty," Edie said, holding up her phone. "I've got some news."

She filled in Penny on the donations and Merriweather's contribution.

"Huh," was all Penny said, her expression impossible to read.

"Bloodline doesn't have to close," Edie stressed.

Before Penny could say anything else, Edie's phone pinged again. Another message from Empty.

"This is popping up all over my socials and might explain some things," the text said, followed by another link.

Edie opened the link. "It's a blog post from Ellora Merriweather," she said, more to herself than to Penny.

Penny took a seat next to Edie and read the blog post alongside her.

> Let me preface this by saying that while I have
> made my living off words, I find it inordinately
> hard to know what to say in this moment. The
> city, and furthermore the world, has learned
> a new truth about existence. Historically,
> when learning about those who are different,
> people have reacted with fear and violence.

There are countless examples of people being othered and victimized for their differences, with each example being a mark of shame in our history. Now is the chance to set aside gut reactions of fear and hate and create a different historical reaction. Now is the chance to face the unknown with courage, curiosity, and empathy.

I have been incredibly fortunate to have my romance novels so embraced by the fine citizens of this city. It has been the highlight of my life to write stories of family and connection and love. That my stories are widely read and so beloved, has given my life meaning.

However, I have often felt as though my words are only embraced so long as they continue to not push any boundaries and uphold a specific image. While many see me as influential in this city, I have always viewed my platform as conditional. This was evident when, as my career as Ellora Merriweather blossomed, my career as E.L. Stormbringer was snuffed out. The vampire series, Nightfall, that I dared to write was met with a much different reception than my home and hearth romance novels. Those books were swiftly banned, though the messages contained in the books were not so different from my other books. The stories still are about family

and connection and love. They are not about
violence or sin, as many have claimed.

I chose to write a vampire series not out
of an allegiance to the occult or a desire to
corrupt the youth in our fine city. I chose to
write a vampire series because, simply put, I
wanted to write something true to me.

I am a vampire.

Edie blinked at the words and tried to make sense of them.
She thought about Ellora Merriweather entering her shop with
the large hat and scarf, and suddenly the criticism she'd received
from Ellora took on an entirely different meaning.

She'd come in for a coffee. Panic had set in when she'd
been recognized, and in that panic she'd tarnished Bloodline's
reputation in an attempt to save herself from being discovered.

Edie continued reading.

I feel an immense amount of panic as I
write those words. People have called me
elusive and mysterious, but the truth is I have
spent many decades hiding the truth about
myself, out of fear of the repercussions of
being honest about my identity.

Speaking up now was never my intention.
However, as others have so courageously put
themselves on the line, I feel compelled to
use my platform to stand beside them.

At the bottom, Ellora had signed her blog post.

Edie turned to Penny, speechless, and tried to decipher the emotions she saw play out across Penny's face.

"Did you know?" she found herself asking.

Slowly Penny nodded. "I'd long suspected," she said. "There had been speculation throughout our community, both that Ellora is one of us and that she'd penned the *Nightfall* series. The night she came into the shop was when it was confirmed for me. She had no pulse, no iron-rich scent of blood."

"You never said anything," Edie commented.

"It wasn't my truth to tell," Penny answered.

Edie understood that. She furrowed her brow as she continued to try to wrap her brain around it all. She thought again about the donations that had been steadily coming in.

"It seems like maybe Ellora changed some people's minds about vampires," Edie said.

"She's always been really influential in this city," Penny agreed.

Edie looked at Penny, hit with a wave of gratitude and love. "Yeah, well, she was influenced by someone else I know."

Penny shrugged off the compliment.

"Sometimes it just takes one voice," Edie said. "One brave soul speaking their truth can, quite literally, change the world."

Bloodline

Edie wasn't sure what to expect from Bloodline's grand re-reopening. The influx of donations toward her coffee shop had indicated that the shop would probably be more widely received than her previous attempt at launching a vampire coffee shop, but the fear of the public's perception was hard to shake after the outcry she'd experienced previously. When she arrived at her shop and saw a mass of people awaiting her, she braced for an angry mob, but the crowd was abuzz with happy chatter, smiles, and excitement, even despite the bitterly cold winter temperatures.

A hush fell over the crowd as she walked past them all and let herself into the coffee shop, locking the door behind her until she was ready to open. She was glad that they had opted to re-create the last reopening, with all four staff being present for the start of the shift. It appeared they'd be needing all hands on deck.

Edie took her time enjoying her final few moments of solitude and quiet. She went to the roasting room where she'd moved her family photos and picked up her favorite photo of her with both of her parents.

"I think, maybe, I've done something really big here," Edie said. "I know the shop is different than what you'd imagined, but I think you'd be really proud of what we're doing here. You'd be proud of the stand that we're making."

Edie could almost feel her parents' hands on her shoulders, and she fought the urge to turn around and look for them. They were gone, but she knew that, at the same time, they were there with her. They'd been there every step of the way, and they'd be there for the real re-launch.

This time, they weren't opening with any false pretense or "for show" gimmick. This time everything was out in the open.

Edie heard the door open, and she set the photo down, going back out to the front of the shop to see Empty and Blake enter together.

"Can you believe this?" Empty asked. She had the biggest smile on her face. She was almost unrecognizable from the melancholic goth girl that had first shown up at Edie's apartment, asking about a seance policy. "Can you really believe this? I mean, look at the crowd!"

"You did this for us," Edie said. "You were the first ones to talk to the media. You got the ball rolling. Then you set up the GoFundMe. You believed in this place when I had no hope left. I can't thank you enough."

Empty shrugged it off like it was no big deal, but a blush colored her cheeks, betraying her feelings.

"It looks like we're the latest commercial craze," Blake grumbled, but Edie noted the sparkle in his eyes. He was as thrilled at their success as the rest of them.

"You were a part of this before it got big," Edie promised. "You can maintain your hipster identity."

"I'm not a 'hipster,'" Blake protested.

Edie was fairly certain that his photo could have been next to hipster in the dictionary, but she didn't argue the point. Chances were their fifteen minutes of fame would run its course soon enough, and things could settle back into a slow, relaxing routine, and Blake could go on pretending to be uninterested in everything "mainstream." And when things settled down, she'd still have her coffee shop, and it could be a local hangout for all the outsiders who needed a place to belong. The Emptys, Sids, and Blakes of the world could keep being their wonderful, quirky selves, and hopefully the vampires in town would even come to see that they had a safe place where they could quietly get coffee with friends.

Edie had never particularly cared for winter before, but the sun now set early in the evening and rose late into the morning, leaving a long stretch of night when Penny didn't have to hide from the world . . . meaning the two could be together.

As such, they didn't have to start the shift without Penny, and Edie lit up when she saw her enter the shop.

"I don't know what to make of all this," Penny said. Her eyes were wide with awe as she looked out the window behind her.

"This is all your act of courage," Edie said. "One act of courage can change the world. You did this. You brought everyone together."

Penny shook her head. "Not me," she argued. "You."

Edie scoffed, but Empty backed Penny.

"It's true," she said. "You're the reason we all came together for this place. You're the reason I went to the media and set up the GoFundMe, and you're the reason Penny came out of the coffin."

Edie swallowed the lump in her throat. "Let's go open those doors," she said. "People are waiting."

Edie opened the door, and the line began to filter into the shop, with the four of them working diligently to fill coffee order after coffee order. Tables were full, so people sat down with friends and strangers alike, making conversation, drinking lattes, and expanding their worldviews. They mostly served human customers, but they did have a few vampire customers take a chance on their little coffee shop.

As it became later in the evening, the immediate rush died down, though a steady stream of customers remained as opposed to their usual empty hours.

As Blake and Empty finished up their shifts, Sid pushed his way into the coffee shop, though he was almost unrecognizable at first. Gone was his black trench coat, replaced instead with a plaid button-down. It also appeared he hadn't shaved in a few days, his face covered with some wispy black stubble.

He waved to everyone and then greeted Empty with a kiss. "You about ready to go, hot stuff? Full moon tonight."

"Let me grab my things from the back," Empty said, and she headed to the roasting room where she'd hung her coat and stored her bag.

"Can I make you a Draculatte for the road?" Edie offered. "My treat this time." She didn't think she and Sid would ever be best friends, but she was thankful for his role in speaking up for her shop, and she wanted the two of them to become friendlier at least.

"Nah," Sid said. "Not my thing."

If Edie had learned anything with Empty and Sid, it was that she should never ask questions, and yet she asked, "No? Why's that?"

Sid leaned forward, propping himself against the counter with his elbows as he leaned in and said in a low, conspiratorial voice, "I realized something about myself lately. I always knew that I was a little different, and I thought that my differences could be explained by vampirism, but that wasn't exactly right. I see that now."

Edie nodded along, not quite sure where he was going with this but certain she was better off in the dark.

"I realized that I'm not a vampire after all," Sid said. "I'm a werewolf. Lycanthropy is a much better fit. It explains my love of night but ability to go outside during the day, my constant hunger, and" he leaned in closer to speak quieter, "my animalistic sexuality."

Edie didn't manage not to cringe.

"It's a full moon tonight," Sid said. "Empty and I are going to head out of town to watch the moon and let those animalistic urges take over."

"Be safe," Edie said as Empty emerged from the back room and linked her arm in Sid's.

She didn't want to think about what those two were going to get up to.

Blake headed out as well, leaving Penny and Edie in charge of the shop on their own. They were too busy for much downtime, but at least the crowd had tapered off enough that they weren't drowning in orders.

When Edie finally had a moment's breather, she leaned back against the counter and watched as Penny steamed the milk for the latte she was making. There was something really sweet and comfortable about the scene, and Edie spoke without giving much thought to her words. They tumbled past her lips with ease.

"I love you; you know that?"

Penny turned to her and smiled, and she looked genuinely

229

happy and at ease in that moment.

"I love you, too."

The chime of the door interrupted their moment and Edie turned. She didn't need to see the woman's face to recognize her. It was the same large hat and flowery scarf she'd worn on her previous visit. Though, this time, when she stepped inside, Ellora Merriweather removed both, not trying to hide her identity.

She approached the counter and extended her hand to Edie. "It's about time we officially meet in person," she said.

Edie didn't take her hand. Instead, she walked around the counter and wrapped Ellora in a large hug.

"Thank you," she said as she stepped back, "for saving my shop."

"You know, sales of my *Nightfall* series are skyrocketing around here? The donation has almost paid for itself."

Edie laughed. "Well, I'm glad to hear it."

Neither of them spoke to any of the larger implications of what had occurred.

"I would like to order a coffee," Ellora said.

Edie smiled, nodded once, and went back around the counter. "What can I get you?" she asked. "On the house."

"Well, I think I need to try one of the Draculattes," with one pump of the O-positive syrup, please."

"Coming right up," Edie promised, and she set to work, making the beverage with one pump of the blood-laced syrup in the coffee mug along with the espresso, before adding perfectly steamed milk. She swirled the microfoam into a few distinct swirls atop the latte and used a pin to pull the microfoam swirls into shape and add details, creating a little bat atop the beverage.

Despite her confidence in her latte abilities, her hand shook a little as she extended the beverage to Ellora.

"It is almost too beautiful to drink," Ellora said.

But she lifted the mug to her lips, her eyes closing as the coffee hit her lips.

"I have waited for the better part of a century to be able to enjoy a coffee out at a coffee shop, and this is even more incredible than anything I could have imagined. What's your secret?"

Edie shrugged.

"There's no secret. I was born into this. It's in my blood."

Acknowledgements

This book began, in a very different form, as an entry for the International 3-Day Novel Contest, which I have competed in for years alongside my best friend, Bryan Mortensen. I'd like to thank everyone involved with 3-Day Novel for putting on this intense writing challenge each year. I also have to thank Bryan, first of all, for encouraging me to take three days away from my other writing projects to write something totally different and fun. A 3-day diversion. Nothing more.

Next, thank you to Sandra Pedler for reading the whimsical little novella that I produced in that over-caffeinated daze and pushing me (and pushing me some more) to do something with this story, even when I doubted the project.

Not sure what to do with a vampire novella, I got in contact with Anna Burke and Samara Breger about writing vampire stories together. I am forever grateful that they decided to join me on this adventure, and that they then abandoned it to grow their stories into the beautiful novels they are. I didn't know my book needed the room to grow, yet here it is now, a full-fledged novel and I can no longer imagine it as anything else. To both of you, I'm consistently inspired by your ways with words and your endless creativity.

Thank you to my editor, Kit Haggard, for tackling a very messy draft of this book and seeing all the possibilities for this story. Your guidance for this book was invaluable, and I so appreciate your ability to somehow see what I'd envisioned for the book behind all the major plot errors.

To my publisher, Salem West, thank you for allowing me to tell stories, and for believing in me when I decided to try my hand at something a little different. Thank you to Ann McMan, for the fun, quirky cover that captures the spirit of the book *perfectly*. And to the rest of the team at Bywater Books who have helped get this book out into the hands of readers—Elizabeth Andersen, Carleen Spry, Cathy Pegau, Toni Whitaker, and Christel Cogneau—thank you all.

D.A. Hartman, thank you for beta reading this book. I appreciated your feedback and support as I fought through the last phases of editing.

And last, but never least, thank you to my wonderful family for being patient with me whenever I take time away to write. A side-effect from writing this book is that my two-year-old now runs around the house shouting *"I a vampire!"*

About the Author

Jenn Alexander is an award-winning author of sapphic romantic fiction from Alberta, Canada. With an M.S. in Counselling, she has a deep interest in learning about people and strives to write character-driven stories. When she's not writing, she works as a psychologist and enjoys dabbling in homesteading hobbies such as bread baking and jam making. She lives on an acreage with her two daughters, two cats, and one dog.

Twitter | @JennAlexWrites
Instagram | jenn.alexander.writes
Facebook | facebook.com//jenn.alexander.313/
Website | https://jennalexander.ca/

Bywater Books believes that all people have the right to read or not read what they want—and that we are all entitled to make those choices ourselves. But to ensure these freedoms, books and information must remain accessible. Any effort to eliminate or restrict these rights stands in opposition to freedom of choice.

Please join with us by opposing book bans and censorship of the LGBTQ+ and BIPOC communities.

At Bywater Books, we are all stories.

We are committed to bringing the best of contemporary literature to an expanding community of readers. Our editorial team is dedicated to finding and developing outstanding writers who create books you won't want to put down.

For more information about Bywater Books, our authors, and our titles, please visit our website.

https://bywaterbooks.com

Printed in the USA
CPSIA information can be obtained
at www.ICGtesting.com
JSHW030401020324
58426JS00003B/5